BLOODGUILTY

... THE CRIME OF TWO CENTURIES ...

**THE PURSUIT OF A MEDICAL MYSTERY
THAT THREATENS TO OVERTAKE OUR PRESENT DAY
SOCIETY AND DESTROY IT
NOT SCIENCE FICTION — SCIENCE FUTURE**

THE TRUE IDENTITY OF JACK THE RIPPER

THE PROOF OF SHERLOCK HOLMES ACTUAL EXISTENCE

WHAT WOULD YOU GIVE TO LIVE A SECOND OR EVEN A THIRD LIFETIME??

A NOVEL BY   Raymond Thor

DANGER PUBLISHING

Westlake Village, California

*When a 100-year-old diary "is found among the possessions of Dr. John H. Watson, and the criminal's identity" (Jack the Ripper) "becomes known to Dave Conway, the narrator of **Bloodguilty**, our icons are in for a smashing."*

-Publishers Weekly

"wide-roving action, and breathless sensationalism"

-The Library Journal

"Like a House of Mirrors curves reality, this thriller bends the calendar. It thrust a modern day Los Angeles snoop and writer into Jack the Ripper's London of 1888, then back again. The plot is alive with intrigue. ...Throughout this thriller, the author mitigates the London fog with luscious scenes in L.A., San Diego, Palm Springs."

-THE BOOK READER

"The same passionate anticipation of the "game afoot" that first welled up in me as a very young man, reading Sir Arthur Conan Doyle's accounts for the first time, rose to the surface as I sped through this adventure. ...an adventure that is truly a non-stop, danger-filled race from the past to the future; ... "Yet, I believe this mystery will be enjoyed by fans of Sherlock Holmes, or fans of any part of the mystery genre birthed by Sir Arthur Conan Doyle."

-Waycross Journal-Herald: 'Bloodguilty'
Good Reading Experience

"True or not, the reader will find himself on both fogenshrouded streets of London's Whitechapel in 1888 and in the deserts of Southern California in 1998."
-The Morgan Messenger

"The author interweaves fact and fiction together so well that the reader is left wondering where one leaves off and the other begins. ... The story is fast moving, spellbinding at times with a slight hint of romance."
-The Chattooga Press

"A mile-a-minute read; I couldn't put it down! The story concept of the 'Ripper' and 'Holmes', combined in past and present is extremely intriguing."
-BOXOFFICE Magazine

"... opens the door into the darkest parts of the human psyche, where the will to live makes even the most horrendous crimes a means to an end. ... Thor manages to capture the rhythms and nuances of Sir Arthur Conan Doyle's Sherlock Holmes and Dr. Watson and transfer those character's essential qualities into two modern characters. Anyone who has ever read a Sherlock Holmes mystery will want to consider picking up a copy of "Bloodguilty". ... you won't want to put it down."
-Argus Observer: "Review: 'Bloodguilty' delves into psyche"

Cover design by: Cynthia Morrell

Dave Conway, a present day writer, is given a diary over 100 years old. It entangles him in a web of evil, deceit, and murder, that threatens his life if he reveals the diary's secrets.

His investigations in pursuit of the truth takes him to the fog enshrouded streets of Whitechapel in 1888 London and continues over 100 years to 1998, in the deserts of Southern California.

Get comfortable in your easy chair, … turn the lights down low, … and … hang on!

BLOODGUILTY

A NOVEL BY **Raymond Thor**

PUBLISHED BY:
DANGER PUBLISHING
1014 S. Westlake Blvd • Suite 14-155
Westlake Village CA 91361-0874 USA

Copyright © 1997   First Printing 1998
Printed in America

Library of Congress Catalog Card Number: 97-68244
Thor, Raymond
    BLOODGUILTY© / Raymond Thor. — 1st ed.
    p.   cm.
    ISBN 0-9658727-6-9
    1. Sherlock Holmes. 2. Jack the Ripper. 3. Science Future.
4. Mystery-Adventure__United States. 5. Authors and publishers__United States. I. Title.

Reg. WGAw

blood·guilt'y (blud'gil'te) adj. Guilty of murder or bloodshed.
blood'guilt', blood'guilt'i·ness n.

Books published by DANGER PUBLISHING are available at quantity discounts on bulk purchases for premium, educational, fund-raising, and special sales use. For details, please write.

This book is dedicated to the following
very special persons

My children who have all their lives encouraged
me to tell and write my stories,
and to my wife and editor,
who puts my words into printed form.

BLOODGUILTY©

AUTHOR'S NOTE:

FACT:

Since 1892, Scotland Yard has retained a sealed file containing all the information from their "Jack the Ripper" murder investigations. It was to be opened in 1992. However, it is my understanding that much of the file is missing ... ... or has been destroyed.

I have utilized many of the actual facts and events concerning the "Ripper" victims along with fictional and real life characters. I have blended them all into a concoction of terror and suspense to stimulate the imagination and curiosity of the reader.

There were moments when the story seemed to write itself. Fiction and historical facts seemed to intertwine so well that the line between the two would fade ... An experience I believe the reader will find terrifyingly real.

Sir Arthur Conan Doyle wrote a Sherlock Holmes story entitled ***The Final Problem*** in which he killed off the famous detective and his nemesis, Prof. Moriarty. The two intellectual equals were in a death struggle above the Reichenbach Falls in Switzerland. Doyle led his readers to believe both men fell into the icy abyss and perished. However, Holmes appeared 3 years later alive and well.

The first part of BLOODGUILTY envisions another explanation surrounding the circumstances of the "final problem" and accounts for the 3 missing years and whereabouts of Sherlock Holmes during that time. So convincing was my account of the lost diary that several friends and readers of the story have asked me if it were true. I explained, "After all, it is just a novel ..." Some did not believe me.

Raymond Thor

EXCERPT FROM THE DIARY
OF DR. JOHN H. WATSON
JANUARY 1892

I have said many times before that he would have been burned at the stake had he lived 200 years prior. It had always seemed to me that his mental powers were without limits. He would often say, "You have seen, Watson, but you did not observe. It is simplicity itself!" Now, at this writing of our greatest and most challenging case, I understand, why of late, his interest has turned to the mysteries of nature. He speaks of becoming a beekeeper in the country ... perhaps it is because this case sits on the pinnacle of his cases... and there is no greater human adventure to come to challenge his talents.

With most sincerest respects to

Sir Arthur Conan Doyle

BLOODGUILTY

A NOVEL BY   **RAYMOND THOR**

"The hour of departure has arrived,
and we go our separate ways -

"I to die and you to live.
Which is better
God only knows —"

                                    - Plato   428-348 BC

CHAPTER 1

LOS ANGELES ... THE PRESENT

The crackling flames in the stone fireplace cast dancing shadows on the walls of the dimly lit cabin. The only other light came from a small kerosene lamp that revealed the silhouette of a man seated at a small table hunched over the paper on which he was intensely writing. An occasional flash of white light revealed black mountain tops through the cabin windows as low rumbling sounds of a dying storm faded into the distance.

"It has been over 100 years since he terrified the entire city of a gaslight London, leaving a legacy of unbridled fear in his bloodthirsty wake.

Jack the Ripper's grisly murders of the East End ladies of the night hardly pales even by today's standards of violence. Is there any woman who walks down a lonely ill-lit street at night who dares to think about Jack without goose pimples erupting from her flesh that send a chill to her heart.

They never caught Jack, but many rumors persist and have surfaced as to his identity and death ... all without proof.

Now, at last, the real story can be told, and it is a story so convoluted in deception and terror that it challenges the reason of a sane man.

A long lost diary was recently delivered to this author that proved to be the property of a Dr. John H. Watson of London. It was inscribed on the cover that the contents not be made public for 100 years after the last dated entry. Having read the diary, I understand better the reasoning of its author... that it be sealed for a century. Perhaps it would have been better if he had never written it at all, for the diary reveals three very disturbing and unsettling propositions.

1. That Sherlock Holmes and Dr. Watson, fictional characters created by Sir Arthur Conan Doyle, actually existed, and that the cases, crimes, and criminals included in their stories existed as well.

2. It reveals the identity of Jack the Ripper.

Holmes, we are told, uncovered a plot so heinous that it was clouded in a dark robe of secrecy that was woven in a cloth of blood and murder. A crime so vast in its undertaking and effects that generations yet unborn would suffer its consequences.

3. And the most disturbing of all three propositions; the diary contains conclusive and irrefutable proof of the first two.

I have decided to chronicle this fantastic story of the sealed diary as quickly as possible. Even now agents acting on behalf of their employers who fear the contents of the diary may be on my trail. Why, you ask, should such possibilities... concern this writer? The answer will become evident as you read further.

My name is Dave Conway. I am a successful professional writer and the story possibilities of the diary have not been overlooked. However, in this instance I am concerned with the truth, whatever it is, and wherever it may lead.

It all began six days ago while I was getting dressed and working on my second cup of morning coffee. The ringing phone caused me to gulp a little as I put the cup down so I could answer it. It was my publisher, Harry Chrysler.

"Hello, Dave? Harry here."

"When did you get back?"

"About 30 minutes ago. I'm still at the airport, but I urgently need to see you. I can be at your place in an hour."

"In about an hour? I was going to write today... so... I'll be here all day. Fine. See you about 10:00 then."

Harry sounded unusually excited, but I dismissed it as my imagination and continued to get dressed, little realizing I was about to become involved in a bizarre set of circumstances that would endanger my life and change a few history books.

I shaved and dressed, then watered the indoor plants. The morning sun made my shoddy bachelor quarters seem bright and slightly orderly; ... out of character for writers who usually have their floor littered with crumpled papers of inept writing. I liked living here in Calabasas; a bedroom community of gated homes and condos, rolling hills, and horse ranches, populated by business professionals in and out of the entertainment industry that like the short commute of a 30-minute ride to LA, Beverly Hills, or Hollywood.

It was another one of those wonderful great-to-be-alive sunny California days. Mid-summer is a little warm in Calabasas, but the ocean breezes coming over the hills from the back door of Malibu cooled the air in the late afternoon. Life was good and the farthest thing from my mind was murder, terror, and fear.

I started going through the mail when I saw Harry's car driving up outside my large picture window. I beat him to the door and opened it just as he reached for the doorbell. "Come on in, Harry..."

He rushed past me with a serious look on his tired and unshaven face as he spoke without looking back.
"... Let's go into the study."

I shut the front door and followed him into my study, where he collapsed into my favorite easy chair, breathing in short bursts. I went over to the bar and poured him three inches of his favorite brandy. "Here! Looks like you need this. I know it's a little early, but you look like you could use an eye opener." He snatched the glass from my hand, drinking as he spoke.

"Thanks. We both might need a Brandy after you hear what I've got to tell you." His voice was strained and shaky, but still strong and vibrant for a man in his early seventies.

"I thought you sounded very serious on the phone. What's wrong, Harry?" I took a seat next to him, hoping it might ease him up a little, but he seemed to get more excitable with each sip of brandy.

"Look, what I'm about to tell you could have far-reaching consequences. It could even be dangerous..."

"You know, Harry, I never thought you had a very big sense of humor. I don't think you're joking. So... if you're not pulling my leg, are you sure you're not exaggerating the situation? I've been telling you for the past two years. Enjoy your golden years. Relax! Retire! You've got it all. Why not slow down? You're working too hard, Old Man!"

A sardonic smile curled up in the corners of his lips as he spoke. "The law says you only need three signatures to be considered certifiable for a mental institution. Maybe after you hear my story, you'll want to be one of the signers. And forget that 'retire' bullshit, I'll have plenty of time to retire when they put me in box city. Now sit down, get a grip, and listen!"

"O.K., I'm listening." I said as I began to hear my own heartbeat.

"You know, of course, of my trip to London last week to attend the Wimbledon Tennis Matches?"

I nodded in the affirmative.

"I had only been in London for two days when Bill Cromwell, an old military acquaintance from the war years, learned of my presence at the tennis matches from a TV commentator who was interviewing a few VIPs from Hollywood and the publishing business.

"Bill had worked in British Intelligence and my assignment as Press Secretary to the American General Staff brought us into contact quite often... we were both a couple of eager shavetail lieutenants and we got to know each other rather well." Another more mischievous smile crossed his face as he was apparently reliving a lusty moment.

"We used to go out with twin sisters and we had some hot times. You can't imagine what it was like during the war years. You weren't even born yet. But our lives were hanging by a thread. We lived each day as if it were the last." He stood up, walked over to the bar for another three inches of brandy, and poured as he spoke.

"Well, after the war we kept in touch for a few years, but eventually we lost contact with each other. I hadn't seen or heard from Bill Cromwell for almost 20 years, so it was quite a shock when he collared me at the local pub in the hotel where we were staying as I was having a nitecap with my daughter, Veronica."

"Say, Mate, do you think the lady has a twin sister you can introduce me to?"

I was startled and stood up, turning to face the voice behind my shoulder. He was a dashing, gray-haired, dapper fellow.

"Well, I can't accuse you of bad taste. Do I know you, sir? ... I don't recall..."

"Don't you know me, Harry? I introduced you to a twin sister once."

"Bill? Bill Cromwell! You twit!" I grabbed his hands and arm. I was delighted to see an old friend.

"VERONICA, this is Bill Cromwell. You heard me speak of him many times. Bill, my daughter, Veronica."

"Your daughter! I should have known you weren't that good of a Casanova." He shook Veronica's hand in a gentlemanly fashion and kissed it ever so slightly.

"How do you do, Mr. Cromwell? My father never stops telling me war stories about the two of you."

"I'll bet he didn't tell you everything!?"

"And I'll bet you're right! I blush easily; but Dad did say you were both a little wild back in those days."

"Sit down and have a drink with us, Bill ... brandy and soda? ...just like the old times."

"Yes, that would do nicely."

I waved to the approaching waiter.

"A Brandy Soda... no ice." Bill smiled at me appreciating my memory of his favorite drink.

"How did you know I was here. I didn't know I was coming myself until Veronica talked me into it at the last minute. We arrived yesterday."

"Yes, I know. ...saw you on the telly today and asked around about where you were staying."

"Listen, Bill. I'm sorry I didn't call you all these years, but I didn't exactly know how to reach you."

"It's all right, Old Chap. My fault, really. I suppose we both just got a little older and less sentimental about old friends. In any case, I'm very glad I was able to catch up with you." He turned to Veronica, cutting off our chatter.

"How are you enjoying the matches, Veronica?"

"Absolutely wonderful. I'm just sorry I can't stay on for a few more days. I'm meeting my husband in Paris tomorrow and returning to New York the day after that. He's there on business, which reminds me I'm getting up early in the morning, so I think I'll retire and leave you and Dad alone to catch up on old times."

"Oh, do you have to leave? Your father and I would be devastated by the absence of your charming presence ... and I didn't intend to intrude on your party."

"Nonsense, Bill! Veronica and I were just having a 'night cap'."

"Good night, Dad! ... Mr. Cromwell!" Bill and I stood up.

I gave Veronica a peck on the cheek, waved goodnight as she left, and sat back down, staring across the table at Bill's melting smile as he took on a more ominous presence. "Bill, it's wonderful to see you ... but is there something wrong? You seem distressed."

"No ... No ... I just ... well, yes there is. It was no accident that I tracked you down this evening to your hotel. It was urgent, as a matter of fact."

"Bill, if it's money or some trouble you're in, I'm in a position to help any way I can."

"No, it's none of those things, it's much more important. Will you meet me tomorrow evening at my club here in London? It is of the utmost importance that you come."

I had never known Bill to be the nervous type, but he seemed very taunt, and his voice was a little shaky as well. Perhaps it was just the years pressing down on him. We were both in the last quarter of our lives. His pleading eyes would not be denied. 'He must be desperate.' I thought.

"I'll have to put off a previous dinner invitation, but, well, of course, I'll come. Anything for an old army buddy, Bill. And I look forward to catching up on the past 20 years."

He took a wallet out of his breast pocket and removed a business-size card, handing it to me as he continued with his instructions. "Here is the address. Any London cabby can take you there. ... 8:30 PM sharp!"

I looked down at the card to see the address. When I looked up, Bill was leaning over the table as he said, "We shouldn't be seen together in public" ... and then he was quickly out the door leaving me a little stunned at his abrupt departure, and alone at my table.

I finished my drink and went upstairs to my room. I was troubled about Bill's last words. It was unlike Bill to leave without the pleasantries of discussing old times. Perhaps he was back with military intelligence and working undercover. I kept rolling the thought around in my mind until sleep put the question to rest.

The following evening I stood outside a fog-enshrouded red brick building ... on which a brass plaque had been inscribed:

THE BAKER STREET SOCIETY

The door was not locked. Upon entering, the decor of the club became Victorian London. The mood was comfortable. Bill came over from across the room, greeting me warmly as he introduced me to one other member.

"Harry! ... my fellow member Charles Potter, the club president."

Pointing out the direction, the president said, "Gentlemen, let's retire to the comfort of the library."

As we walked, Bill pointed out Holmes' memorabilia: books, original drawings, pipes, and newspaper stories. We entered a dark wood-paneled room decorated with oil portraits of Holmes, Watson, and Villains ... We seated ourselves around a very large table surrounded by six plump red leather chairs etched with brass studs.

Mr. Potter walked over to a small bar and brought back three glasses and a brandy bottle. "Have a brandy, Mr. Chrysler. I'm bartender this evening. You will note the absence of members or staff. The club is dark tonight. We wanted complete privacy for this meeting." He waved his free hand toward the walls of library books and memorabilia. "As you can see we are the Keepers of the Flame. We both guard and insure the immortal continuance of the world's greatest consulting detective and his faithful chronologist, Dr. Watson. All of us here, and others, have sworn to this oath." He finished pouring three drinks, handed me a glass, sat down and pushed a drink across the table to Bill.

"Yes, I've heard of your organizations, but, Holmes and Watson are fictional characters. Should not your true homage be to Sir Arthur Conan Doyle, their creator?" I said.

Mr. Potter smiled, apparently anticipating my question as he said, "Yes, of course. But you see, the club holds a theory that much of what Doyle wrote was fact and that he himself may have been either one or both Sherlock Holmes, and Dr. Watson; a split personality or several personalities inhabiting one mind and body. We are not alone in that theory. But the most popular theory by many critics and scholars supposes that Holmes actually existed, but to protect his effectiveness, worked under another name and that Doyle was, in fact, Dr. Watson. He was a medical doctor. He was also considered to be eccentric due to his personal peculiarities with spiritualists. It was common knowledge. So, the theories are not without foundation. He was a brilliant and unusual man. However, we here at The Club are dedicated and devoted to his work and memory; whoever he may have been."

"Bill, do you honestly mean to say you believe Sherlock Holmes may have actually existed, and that all his cases actually happened?"

"Yes. I do! We all do!"

"Well, good manners should preclude my playing Devil's Advocate, here in your own club and to your fellow member, but I can hardly resist... If what you say is true, how do you account for the silence of his clients when the accounts of his cases appeared in publication?"

"Simple." said Mr. Potter. "Discretion in Victorian times was essential. The slightest hint of scandal was enough to destroy ... a career ... a marriage ... and indeed one's entire life. You are the business representative and publisher of one of the most notable American authors on Historical Exposes. You know the advantage of changing a few minor details here and there to thinly disguise people, places, and events so as to avoid litigation and embarrassment ... and don't forget ... it pays to advertise. In that time ... people in high places ... knew where to go for help ... and further ... could count on Holmes' personal discretion."

"All right. All that you say makes sense, but you still haven't proven anything."

Bill sported a broad grin as he spoke, "That's why you're here, Harry, because Mr. Potter and myself now have irrefutable proof that Sherlock Holmes, or whatever name he used, actually existed."

There was a heavy silence as the room seemed to close in on me.

Mr. Potter spoke first. "I have decided to take you into our confidence because Bill will vouch for your honesty and discretion; presumably you are an honorable man ... and most important because you have a direct personal connection to a highly successful American writer."

Bill placed his hand on my arm as he said, "The opportunity presented itself to us when I saw you on the telly and felt surely the hand of providence was at work. Now there only remained the bold task of deciding a proper course of action on the club's recent discovery, and the details that have led to a discovery so vast, its implications and future effects upon the world can only be guessed.

I was not prepared for Bill's intensity, but he held my attention.

"Harry, you remember the London Blitz during the war. The German's relentless bombing of the city left many buildings in ruins.; in particular, one personally owned residence of Doyle which was sold shortly after his death in 1930. It remained intact and stood undisturbed until it was severely damaged by bombs in 1942. It laid in ruins until 1948 - 3 years after the war. The Baker Street Society heard of the property and its condition. It was about to be cleared for development of an apartment building.

"Naturally, the Society wouldn't hear of such a desecration. So, with a determined spirit and a lofty cause, they raised the money to buy the property and to have it restored to its former Victorian glory which you now see and appreciate. Naturally, repairs and continued maintenance are necessary to keep up its impeccable appearance. The money comes from the membership and donations from devoted fans of the master worldwide.

"Recently, ... we were required by fire code to reconstruct several areas in the basement and in doing so uncovered a small portion of the original structure ... a storage closet that was covered in the bombing and completely overlooked by its previous owners ... along with its contents ... until now! Inside were a few authentic items of its time ... obviously over 100 years old ... oil lamps, candles, matches, paper, and most important, a wooden sealed box containing a leather-bound diary, wrapped in a rubber material, which you see here on the table." He pointed to an ornately carved wooden box in the center of the table. I had thought it contained chess pieces or cigars.

"Now, at this point in our story we must have your absolute discretion... your oath of secrecy if you should decide not to become involved..." The smile melted off Bill's face; he was dead serious.

I paused for a few seconds, then picked up the gauntlet. "You have it! I said. "Continue! I'm in too deep and ... my curiosity ... wouldn't let me sleep if I stopped now."

Bill opened the lid of the box, reached in, unfolded a soft cloth and took out an old leather-bound book. "Very well. This book is a diary written and signed by a Dr. John H. Watson of Baker Street, London. It includes dated entries in the year of 1888 and the last entry, you will note, is engraved on the cover: 'Not to be made public before January 30, 1992 ... 100 years from the last entry.'"

I examined the cover of the diary, fascinated with the prospect of holding a bit of history in my hands. "But how can you be sure of its authenticity, or when it was written."

"Harry, you know I was in British Intelligence during the war and for some time after. Many of the club's members have civil service connections. Samples of the diary ... paper, ink, leather ... have been examined by experts who didn't know what the diary contained. And all tests ... chemical, carbon-dating, ultrasonic, microscopic... are conclusive. The paper, ink, and leather have been dated back at least 100 years. There is no doubt about its age or authenticity. It proves conclusively that Holmes existed. It is in Doyle's own handwriting."

"No, Bill. It only proves that Sir Arthur Conan Doyle could have written it 100 years ago."

"It proves much, much more, than that, Harry. It tells us the identity, and purpose, of one of history's most dreaded fiends ... Jack the Ripper. An actual person ... not a fictional character. and ... coincidentally, it is a fact that the Scotland Yard files on the "Ripper Case" were sealed for 100 years: 1892-1992. However, it appears much of the files are missing or have been destroyed."

I was stunned. The realization slowly set in. I was not sure if it was all a joke ...or real. I looked down at the diary. 'Hell!' I thought. 'A little danger at my age would probably be preferable to dying of boredom.' Bill asked me to read the diary and learn the irrefutable truth. I took the diary and seated myself in a comfortable chair. I fumbled to find my eyeglasses in my breast pocket and began to read... as the clock on the fireplace struck 9 PM.

As I closed the last page of the diary, the clock struck 11 PM. I took out my handkerchief and wiped my brow and stammered out loud to the others. "My God!!! It is true!? Is it possible... ?"

I took a long drink, struggling with shaky hands to keep from dropping the glass, as Bill put his hands on my shoulders to steady me for the moment. "Harry, we have a plan and would like to offer you a part in it that will be of incredible importance and of great profit to us all.

"First, you agree to take the diary and leave the country at once and attempt to publish the story; the world has the right to know the true facts.

"Second, a fair share of the publishing rights and fees go to the Society for its continued existence—its cash flow is fluid as cement, so the funds are sorely needed.

"Third, security is essential as we may all be endangered if certain forces become aware our plans; every cause has its detractors. That is why I left you so abruptly Last night.

Mr. Potter stood up from the table and leaned forward toward me as he spoke. "The Society has microfilm copies of the diary and will take the chance on it leaving the country ...as the police and government could be a problem. Will you help us, Mr. Chrysler?!"

My mouth failed to open. The words were there, but I couldn't seem to get them out. Finally a soft hissing 'Yes' passed from my lips.

The late morning sun struck the empty glass giving off a laser bright light blast to my eyes. It was enough to bring me back to the present moment as Harry recounted the end of his story.

"My plane left London the next morning and I came here straight from the airport. Dave, you and I have to work on this together."

"Well, to say the least, I'm more than slightly astounded... and curious, about what's in that diary that could be so conclusive as to convince you of its authenticity. Why did the Society choose me?"

"Dave, you're the best damn investigative writer in the business, and your name on a book means sales. Thanks in no small part to the marketing efforts of your publisher, me.

"Hell! ... Read the diary and convince yourself. If you do, you're sworn to secrecy and made aware of the possible danger. And ... not to be overlooked ...

"We'll all make a lot of money!"

The whole thing sounded crazy, but Harry Chrysler was not a flippant man. If he thought there was a pony underneath all this horse shit, then he would be determined to dig it out.

I stood up and slowly paced the floor thinking, as Harry took the diary from his briefcase ... it was wrapped in a soft brown cloth.

Harry unwrapped it and handed it to me. One could clearly see the aging quality of its cover ... the odor of antiquity was evident. I walked back to my desk, and paused to study the rich brown leather binding which was still remarkably soft to the touch. I could envision a distraught and tired Watson setting down the words in a Victorian setting ... perhaps by gaslight. I suppose I was relating to the writer ... one of considerable credentials.

I opened the cover to the first page, brown with age but clearly very readable in a smooth handwritten style that shouted out the date of the first entry ... November 1, 1888.

My mind's eye peered deep into the smoky veil of time which cleared as I read on.

"This beastly bastard must be stopped at any price ... He has butchered these depraved ladies of the night who, although immoral, do not deserve the fiendish desecration of their bodies."

CHAPTER 2

THE DIARY ... LONDON 1888

It was an unappetizing murder story that appeared in the morning paper while both Holmes and I engaged in our ritual breakfast prepared by Mrs. Hudson in our digs at Baker Street.

The third and fourth Ripper murder victims in recent days were two ladies of questionable character who apparently, while plying their trade on the dark streets of Whitechapel, met their untimely end at the hands of a fiend who did not even possess the rudimentary talents of a common butcher, hence the "Ripper" title given the murders by the newspapers, the latest murders were described as a double event, committed perhaps within minutes of each other.

Holmes seemed unconcerned and when I solicited his opinion of the story, he simply stared off into space, saying very little.

"Interesting, but there's more to come from such a creature. They usually are tortured souls seeking a retribution of sorts. Well, come along, Watson, we'll be late for our fencing exercises."

"Must we? Really, Holmes, you are contrary. One moment you sit still for days pondering the mysteries of the universe, ...the next moment you're up and about like a shot."

"The mind and body, Watson, must compliment each other. Now be a good fellow and hurry. We can drop off your pocket watch at the jeweler on the way."

"Now, how did you know I intended to drop off my watch at the jeweler? Wait, don't tell me. I'll deduce the answer myself.

"A. I usually wind my watch at the breakfast table." Holmes nodded approvingly.

"B. And since I did not this morning, you would have assumed I forgot to do so or that it was broken. Why not forgotten?"

Holmes scooped up his coat and hat from the chair that he had deposited it on in such a cavalier manner the evening before and took my coat off the coat rack, handing it to me as he spoke.

"Because, my dear fellow, I noticed that you twice looked at the clock on the mantelpiece to confirm the time, and knowing how you are meticulous about your appointments, it seemed odd that you did not take out your pocket watch for a comparison. Therefore, the watch must be malfunctioning and that's why you didn't wind it this morning. Further, you wound it yesterday, and usually a watch of such great sentimental value - which you told me about yourself - is repaired without delay."

I have said many times before that he would have been burned at the stake had he lived 200 years prior. It had always seemed to me that his powers were without limits.

He would often say, "You have seen, Watson, but you did not observe. It is simplicity itself!"

Now, at this writing of our greatest and most challenging case, I understand, why of late, his interest has turned to the mysteries of nature. He speaks of becoming a beekeeper in the country ... perhaps it is because this case sits on the pinnacle of his cases... and there is no greater human adventure to come to challenge his talents.

We entered the men's athletic club and changed into our fencing gear. Holmes is an accomplished swordsmen with the saber. We began to cross swords, moving about swiftly, paring, while exchanging daring words of 'Bravado' and insults common to the male ego. Although Holmes is the scholar and thinker, he is a physical creature as well and fairly athletic.

As a former military man having served in Afghanistan and India in Her Majesty's Service, I could very easily keep up the pace. He almost had me at his convenience several times, but each time I avoided the final blow, reversing the advantage in spite of an old shoulder wound.

We continued our workout as a servant steward awaited a break in the action to deliver a message to Holmes. "Mr. Holmes, a gentleman in the foyer wishes to speak to you. I regret the interruption, but he said it was most urgent."

Holmes walked to the outer hall where a distinguished gentleman of high office waited. Before the man could complete his first sentence, Holmes deduced the reason for his visit.

"Mr. Holmes, my name is Walter Crenshaw. I have come on a most urgent errand. ...."

"Yes, I know, the Whitechapel business. The home office must find it quite distressing to request my assistance... and your recall from the foreign service in India."

"But how could you know the purpose of my mission. I only left the Home Office 1 hour ago... and my recall... ?"

Holmes responded with a staccato rhythm as he obviously enjoyed the moment and the prospect of an interesting adventure. He walked in circles around the young man as if he were studying a horse for a possible purchase.

Crenshaw was forced to turn about one way and then another as Holmes continued his movements, while he pointed his finger at various locations of the young man's body and clothing.

"By observation and deduction. Your dark suit, so favored by the foreign service, with its quality fabric, can hardly be purchased by the middle class who can ill afford such finery these days."

Holmes stopped long enough to gently touch the fabric of the coat with his thumb and forefinger. "The weave of the material is peculiar even to the naked eye; it is manufactured in India, and, I understand, most sought after and in vogue. Your school tie; Eaton, I believe?"

"Yes! " he stammered as Holmes continued.

"... tells us of your educational qualifications for the work. The true complexion of your skin color is evident by the much lighter color of the skin behind the ear areas indicating you have acquired a deep tan. And since English sunshine has been somewhat scarce these past few weeks, it is obvious you acquired it elsewhere. The yellow color in the white of your eyes indicates a recent bout with the River Fever presently pervading the Bihar Province of India.

"And if all that were not enough, your right wrist has a lighter strip of tanned surface which I noticed when we shook hands, indicating a band of sorts was worn there from time to time. Foreign service personnel often act as couriers with handcuffed briefcases attached to their wrists. Ergo, you are found out."

Holmes spun around again, compelling the young man to move in dizzying circles. "You did not follow us here or the urgency of the matter would have caused you to interrupt our journey. Therefore you must have inquired at our domicile on Baker Street. Mrs. Hudson has instructions not to give anyone information beyond our expected return, so you must have impressed her with your government credentials which caused a modest dereliction of her duties.

"Further, I have been of service to the home office and government in the past, and this "Ripper" matter is causing some consternation in parliament. I have also been pondering the matter the past few days and have been expecting an inquiry."

If I had not seen Holmes perform these logical deductions on several occasions, I would most certainly have been astounded as was the young Mr. Crenshaw, who now was able to speak as Holmes took a momentary repose.

"Mr. Holmes, I am overwhelmed. I had heard of your reputation and you can believe me when I say these recommendations still understate your talents which I have just seen displayed. Now I am sure we will very quickly get to the end of this "Ripper" business."

"On that I concur! You have a carriage waiting, I presume."

"Yes, Sir! Right out front!" replied the happy Mr. Crenshaw, anxious and obviously pleased with the results of his errand.

Holmes turned and walked to the dressing room as I followed. He spoke to Crenshaw without turning back. "We will make ourselves presentable and be with you shortly."

As our carriage approached the front gate of Scotland Yard, we drove past a roving group of men which would be better described as an angry mob of ruffian types; some throwing garbage at the dozen or so Bobbies guarding the gate; others carrying placards with large red lettering presumably representing the blood of the victims: "Devil! Killer!" ... We could hear their angry shouts. "We are not for butchering. We live down at Whitechapel. We'll catch and lynch the Ripper if you can't!!"

We drove to the rear gated entrance of the Yard which also had a respectable presence of Bobbies guarding the closed gates, but no angry mobs as yet. The gate opened just enough to clear our carriage. For a moment I had doubts about clearing the narrow opening. The constables, upon recognizing Mr. Crenshaw, passed us through without a pause in the movement of our galloping horses. The gate opened and closed in one smooth motion, and in an instant the carriage came to an abrupt halt at a nondescript entrance … which was most likely used for arrested felons.

Mr. Crenshaw sprung up and out the door, beckoning us to follow. We entered the darkened hallway and climbed up what can only be described as a slightly tilted ladder. We emerged into the upper administrative offices. We picked up the pace behind Crenshaw who slowed and then stopped in front of a closed door, knocking softly as he loudly whispered, "He is here, Mr. Secretary."

The door opened and we followed Crenshaw into the room. The large man seated behind the small wooden desk and the other rather tall gentlemen facing a smoky window, made the dark room appear even more compressed and stifling than it was. He stood up and came around the desk as he spoke, "Thank you for coming so quickly Mr. Holmes … Mr. Watson, you know the Chief Inspector, of course?" He pointed to the man who did not turn from the window and overlooked his lack of courtesy by continuing without a pause. "I would like to say it is nice to see you both again, but useless amenities are out of place for the moment." ....

I recognized him at once. It was the Home Secretary. We shook hands as we exchanged greetings. His solemn mood greatly increased, making him seem older then his 50 years.. "Terrible! .... Terrible! .... Ungodly!! ...... He must be stopped Mr. Holmes . There are riots in the streets, demonstrations, panic …, mobs lynching anyone that looks or acts suspicious." ..... neighbor against neighbor.

He turned toward the only other glass window in the room, peering out as if looking for the murderer. "I'm sorry I could not meet you at the Government House in official and more dignified offices, but discretion and secrecy is of the utmost importance.

Holmes quick grasp of the situation immediately reassured the Secretary that he understood his reasoning. "I agree entirely Mr. Secretary, and we must act swiftly if we are to prevent any further murders. I presume you wish my assistance in the matter and will arrange for me to have complete access to all the evidence, the coroners reports, the murder sites, and if possible, the bodies themselves. I work alone and will provide you with information that I have completely analyzed and is pertinent to the case. I must review any witness testimony, and photographs." Holmes ran his fingers along the stacks of papers on the side table.

The Chief Inspector, who had not yet withdrawn his attention from looking out the window, slowly turned, as he said. "I must be frank, Mr. Secretary. I am opposed to any outside investigators participating in what I consider a police matter, and I take it as a personal affront to the talents of the entire police staff."

He then turned to Holmes and myself, continuing his opposition to our assistance. "I apologize, Mr. Holmes, if I have offended you, there is nothing personal in my rejection of your assistance."

One could see the Home Secretary's exasperation with the Inspector's objections was clearly at the breaking point. His face flushed a dark red as he spoke. "Chief Inspector, I am days, perhaps hours, away from being asked to submit my resignation to the Prime Minister ... and I can assure you in that event you will join me amongst the people who have lost their situation. I am not going to sit here and listen to this dribble about police morale while the women of Whitechapel are being butchered. This beastly bastard must be stopped at any price. He has butchered these depraved ladies of the night who, although immoral, do not deserve this fiendish desecration of their bodies."

The Secretary opened the black file folder on the desk. Taking a sheet of paper with one hand as he put on his eye spectacles with the other, he began to read to us softly at first, but with the growing intensity of a building storm. "Polly Ann Nichols, murdered on Buck's Row Street, August 31, 1888.

"The murdered woman was found lying on her back; her legs straight out as if the murderer had posed her for a picture. Her eyes open, her throat had been cut ear to ear, severing the arteries back to the spinal cord. She was dressed in rusty brown Ulster with seven brass buttons, a dark dress, 2 flannel petticoats marked with the words of the maker, 'Lam Beth Work House'.

"Outside of her clothes the police found only 2 possessions on her body: a black comb and a broken piece of looking glass. She had been completely disemboweled. The killer's knife was driven into the lower abdomen and ruthlessly continued up to the upper chest. Further slashes on the body were noticeable along with several stab wounds on the upper body and vagina. The weapon of choice was speculated to be a long-bladed knife. There were bruises on the neck and face indicating a possible blow."

He slowly placed the report down on the desk as he walked to the window, speaking out his inner thoughts rather than to us. "She was an alcoholic and a prostitute and a member of the thousands of poverty-stricken people that populate the East End and the Whitechapel area. She was all these things, but most of all she was unlucky because she met The Ripper, a fiend from Hell, and this past week he has mailed the remains of a human kidney to the police to further taunt us." With that final crescendo of verbiage the Secretary fell back into the desk chair drained.

We stood frozen for the moment, still trying to remove the ghastly picture from our minds that the Secretary had put there.

The Chief Inspector turned to Holmes as he said, "Please accept my apologies, Mr. Holmes..., Mr. Secretary... Of course, you're entirely correct. These murders must cease. I seemed to have lost sight of my obligations. If you wish my resignation ..." The Home Secretary cut him off.

"Nonsense, Inspector, you are just frustrated and exhausted, as are all of us who have attempted to stop this madman."

"I agree entirely with the Home Secretary, Inspector." Holmes said. "The dead are not the only victims in this ugly business. I assure you that both Dr. Watson and myself will in no way compromise your present investigation, but I will need your cooperation."

"You will have it, Mr. Holmes!" he replied.

The Home Secretary, now satisfied that we were all in agreement, concluded the meeting with a brisk exit from the room, as he said. "All the 'Ripper' files are available for your examination, but must not leave this room. You will have access to it 24-hours a day. Mr. Crenshaw and the Inspector will provide all that you require, Mr. Holmes. I will expect to hear of your progress as quickly as possible. Help us stop this ungodly creature. Good day, Gentlemen!"

We stayed in that claustrophobic room for several more hours as Holmes studied stacks of files at least three feet tall.

Upon returning to our rooms at Baker Street, we found that Mrs. Hudson had provided us a welcome cup of tea and sandwiches for a late lunch; and for which I was very thankful . We ate before we read the second murder file on which Holmes had made copious notes.

The second body was found on September 8, 1888, a little after 6 AM at the back of a house; 29 Hamburg Street. Her name was Annie Chapman. She, too, was a lady of ill repute and fortune. She was last seen alive at 5:30 AM with a man. She was strangled, slashed across her face, and disemboweled. The Municipal Police lacked much of the detail and scientific approach to murder that Holmes practiced, and in doing so may have overlooked many clues. The murdered woman carried a comb and a paper case.

The killer had laid two of her rings and some pennies and farthings at her feet. Near her head was part of an envelope and a piece of paper containing 2 pills. On the back of the envelope was the seal of the Sussex Regiment and on the other side, the letter "M" and a postmark: 28 Aug. 1888. ... and now two more murders.

We had spent hours going through mounds of reports and witness statements. Holmes mind was reeling in clues as he began the arduous task of piecing the puzzle together, and in disregarding the multitude of false information and clues being received by the police daily.

The next day proved to be even more interesting and informative for we were to meet with the coroner and inspect the actual murder scenes ... which were still being guarded by constables who were to keep morbid curiosity seekers from destroying or taking souvenirs and any items that might be useful evidence.

Holmes worked late into the night studying the crime reports, and mounting small slips of paper notes onto a large square board. He would place a note on the board, step back to review the whole board, then step forward to examine a small part. Finally he would seat himself into his chair and smoke a cigarette and begin the process all over again.

He would stare at the board for what seemed like endless hours, sometimes leaning forward to peer through the billowing smoke as if seeing something on the board for the first time. At other times he played his violin which I found particularly soothing on occasion. Holmes was an accomplished musician. He had many talents ... science, chemistry, and some limitations ... astronomy and women.

The only woman he seemed enamored with was one who bested him in the Scandal in Bohemia case. He would only refer to her as 'the woman', but his tone of voice was always respectful and sincere.

It had been a disturbing day and I was physically exhausted, I did not retire until midnight ... leaving Holmes to his thoughts and his crime board.

The coroner's office was close to Scotland Yard. We had been there on previous occasions when investigating subjects of other cases about which I have written. However, I will not depart from the present investigation to engage in old business.

The coroner, Dr. Macintosh, greeted us in his working apron covered with bloody stains; some still wet. He engaged us in the expected small talk for a moment, but Holmes was quick to the point and impatient about getting down to the business at hand ... the Whitechapel slaughters.

"Doctor, in reading your medical reports I was curious to note your opinion about the surgical talent of The Ripper on one hand, and your comparison to him as a clumsy butcher on the other. Are not these views diametrically opposed to each other?"

The doctor was up to questions and said, "They are, Mr. Holmes, but when you see the last two victims' bodies for yourself ... which we still have on the examining table ... I believe Dr. Watson will endorse my opinion." He invited us to join him in the Examiner's Room.

The odor of the dead and rotting corpses as we entered the room was not unexpected, as I said we had been here before. As a medical doctor this was not as unsettling to me as I think it was to Holmes, who although a professional and having experience with the dead, showed great restraint and self-control.

Upon standing before the covered corpses of The Ripper's two victims, I was to rethink those thoughts. The doctor slowly peeled back the blood-stained sheets to reveal the ghastly sight of a completely disemboweled body of what appeared to be a female. It was difficult to tell from the numerous slashes of the knife to the face and body. Even my experience as a medical officer with the dead and wounded in the Afghanistan War did not prepare me for this sight. The second body was similarly disfigured.

I examined the wounds more closely. I said, "I can see why you made those contradicting statements. Holmes, he is quite right. See here where the uterus and other organs were cut out. Clean, surgical cuts, ... and yet ... these other areas were slashed and torn as if by a wild animal. It is perplexing to say the least."

The coroner smiled, obviously pleased on being exonerated

before the great Sherlock Holmes. He pointed to a particular wound, soliciting our opinion. "What do you make of this cut, Mr. Watson ... Mr. Holmes?"
It was a deep cut upward in the vagina to the navel. We moved closer as Holmes pondered.

"Very neat and clean. A very cautious cut, as if avoiding damaging the uterus underneath. ... Hello! What's this? Bruises on both wrists? This means she was alive at the moment, being held by a very strong person ... or persons."

"You mean there could be more than one murderer involved, Mr. Holmes?'

"It is possible, but let's not jump to any conclusion just yet. She wore rings on two of her fingers. See the lighter area of the skin. Do you have them, doctor?"

No, Mr. Holmes, we found no rings. Now if you have no further need of me I have more pressing duties. You may, if you wish, continue your examination of the bodies. Gentlemen!" He turned and left Holmes and I standing there as he left through swinging doors.

I couldn't help but think the work had made the man callous and indifferent, perhaps a necessary emotional buffer to protect one's sanity.

We continued our examination after finding two pairs of rubber gloves. We turned the bodies over and examined them from back to front, head to foot. Several curious things were noted: a front tooth repaired; the dental work was sloppy, apparently a cheap work for little money, needle marks on one arm...drugs?...or perhaps medication? Finally, the air was too thick to breathe and we left with many more questions unanswered than when we arrived.

"I suspect, Watson, we are in for an extended investigation of the case. There is a sinister force behind these murders; a very powerful sinister force."

CHAPTER 3

THE MURDER SCENES

We arrive at the Buck's Row murder scene, a street in close proximity to a slaughter house on one side and London Hospital and a Jewish cemetery on opposite sides.

The Chief Inspector was already there awaiting our arrival with an impatient indifference. He walked toward our carriage just as it came to an abrupt stop ... all the while talking as he awaited for us to alight from the carriage. "Mr. Holmes! Dr. Watson! If you will follow me, Gentlemen." He turned, not waiting for a reply, and walked brusquely in the side alley, stopping midway. He pointed to the ground ... in front of the ally's side wall ... not looking up as he spoke, "'Ere's where we found the body, Mr. Holmes. You can still see the dried blood stains."

We started toward the body that was no longer there, but I must confess I could see her lying there with those horrible wounds inflicted on her frail body.

Holmes, of course, was beyond this type of reverie. He was engrossed in the problem ... detached from the horror of it all ... to him it was a puzzle to be solved. He examined every inch of the ground, the wall ... He moved up the alley toward the sound of barking dogs coming from the slaughter house. He kept walking toward the incessant barking ... coming to a gated metal fence.

Two very large and dangerous looking hounds leapt toward Holmes, biting the iron bars with their saliva dripping jaws. There was no doubt that ... had the fence not been there ... Holmes or anyone else unfortunate enough to pass by would be torn to pieces.

I shouted out to him, keeping my distance and a firm grip on my revolver inside my coat pocket, "Careful, Holmes! Don't get too close." I yelled out as a tall man came from within the slaughterhouse and into the darkening light of the late afternoon sun.

"'Ere, get away from the fence there, Gov'ner.", he yelled. "You're making my dogs a bit tight in the ass. Move on before I turn 'em loose." He paused to wipe his blood stained hands on his apron. He was a large man with a facial scar on his cheek, reminiscent of the famous Heidelberg saber scar so proudly worn by the Austrian elitist. He gritted his teeth, and for a moment it was difficult to see the difference between the foaming saliva mouths of his dogs or their master.

Holmes moved directly toward the man. "Do you keep these animals outside all night ... free to roam the yard?!"

"What business is it of yours?!" He started to unlock the gate as the Inspector and myself moved forward with our revolvers drawn. He stopped in his tracks, as Holmes seemingly oblivious to the action, continued to examine the ground just inside the fence ....

"Hold on, Gov'ner. I didn't mean any harm." He spoke as he backed up with his hands raised. "I didn't know the gentleman was on police business."

Two more uniformed constables came running toward us, momentarily attracting the dogs attention while Holmes very quickly stretched his arm in-between the bars, scraping up some brown stains on the ground.

The dogs were quick to see the action and only the interference of their owner prevented the vice-like bite of one dog that surely would have removed several of Holmes' fingers. I pulled him back by the shoulders, setting him in a backward stumble from his loss of balance, from which he was able to recover.

"Mr. Holmes," the Inspector sneered pointing to his head, "Are you a bit bent upstairs? Those animals are killers!"

Holmes was busy putting the brown scrapings into a slip of paper and folding it carefully and placing it in his vest pocket as he patronized the Inspector with an apology for the inconvenience. "Yes! Of course! Careless of me. My apologies to you, Gentlemen. And thank you all for your prompt response."

He turned and once again repeated the question to the butcher. "The dogs ... are they free to run the yard at night?"

The butcher hesitated, not quite sure if he should answer, apparently thinking he might be breaking some laws on dog restraints.

"Come, now, man. Let's have it. You will not be troubled by us any further for a truthful answer..", Holmes said.

"Well, sometimes ... Yes! They are free to run about the place ... but only for protection against robbers. Honest, Gov'ner, we 'ave been robbed three or four times this past year, and ..."

"Thank you!" Holmes said, abruptly turning and walking back into the alley. We all followed as the butcher stood there with his jaw hung slacked in the puzzlement of it all ... just like the rest of us.

The Inspector yelled out as we followed. "Will that be all for this crime area, Mr. Holmes?"

Holmes yelled back without turning. "Quite! Let's move on to the Chapman murder site at Lanbury Street."

Holmes and I returned to the carriage and seated ourselves on opposite sides. I was about to inquire about his actions at the butcher yards fence when the Inspector stepped into our carriage and said, "Do you mind if I ride along with you, Gentlemen?"

"Not at all!", Holmes replied. We signaled the driver to proceed as the Inspector started to speak.

"Mr. Holmes, as you know, I was personally and professionally against your invitation into this case by the Home Secretary. ... even so, if it helps us to capture this madman I would be grateful. But, Sir, your methods are strange to me and that incident with the dogs ..." Holmes interrupted.

"I understand and appreciate your position Inspector and I am aware that my actions might seem strange to someone else ... but let me ask you this? Did you not learn something more about the murder?"

"What could we learn? We already knew about the butcher. He was our first suspect due to the proximity of the slaughter house to the crime, and his apparent qualifications with knife and cleaver. But his alibis were confirmed. At the time of the murders he was seen drinking in a local Pub all evening until he fell into a drunken stupor at 2 in the morning. We are still watching his movements, however."

"Did you not observe another possibility?

"What possibility would that be, Mr. Holmes?" asked the Inspector. I also felt the need to join the Inspector in his curiosity.

"Perhaps, Inspector, Mr. Holmes will enlighten us both. What did you see, Holmes?"

"The dogs, Gentlemen! The dogs are the key to part of the mystery. Observe that their incessant barking continued throughout our visit to the murder site."

"Yes!" I replied, "Unless you were a deaf man ... but what is there to learn from that?"

"Much! For instance in reviewing all the witness statements and neighbors in the vicinity, none reported hearing the barking dogs. That would suggest to you that the butcher's dogs did not bark because they knew the killer; perhaps their master.

"But his alibi would compel us to seek the answer elsewhere. I would wager that the dogs were drugged with salted meat thrown to them through the fence ... "

"I see ...", said the Inspector. "That was the reason for your scraping the spots on the ground.?"

"Exactly. And when I examine them with chemicals, I'll wager I find the remnants of a sleeping potion used by medical doctors during amputations, to calm the nerves." His suspicion was confirmed later when he made chemical tests of the red material. "There is more to learn ... much more!"

"How so?" said The Inspector.

"I suggest that the murderer was not searching the area like a predator looking for a spontaneous target of opportunity, but rather that the time, place, and the meeting of the victim was planned in advance ... perhaps a sexual rendezvous? Yet ... this piece of the puzzle raises more questions. Why take the risk of arranging a rendezvous?"

"Why would he choose that particular location?" asked the Chief Inspector.

"Perhaps, because it affords dim lighting and an excellent side alley for uninterrupted privacy and a very good escape route on either end should he be caught in the dastardly act. Remember, our murderer requires both time and privacy to inflict his mutilations; at least ten to fifteen minutes, according to Dr. Watson's experienced evaluation of the victims."

We all sat in thoughtful silence pondering this new information as the carriage came to a stop at Lanbury Street. The Inspector looked puzzled but dismissed Holmes' theory with a wave of his hand as he stepped from the carriage.

We joined him in a dark corner of the street where the late afternoon light was dimming by the minute. I put my hand into the inside of Holmes' arm, slowing our pace, as I whispered. "Was that wise? ... to tell the Inspector what you think?"

"Unwiser yet, if I did not! Besides, he will not veer from his planned course. I can only hope my suggestion and information did not fall on deaf ears. However, I expect to know more over the next few days. I suspect, Watson, we are in for an extended investigation of the case. There is a sinister force behind these murders; a very powerful sinister force."

The thought chilled me to a shudder … or was it the late afternoon dampness creeping into my bones. I had hoped to get on with this last piece of business quickly and retire to our rooms for a welcomed cup of tea laced with whiskey.

At Lanbury Street, the scene was similar; a dark alcove just beyond Hamburg Street, close to Spitalfields Market, Millers Court, and the Christ Church.

Holmes once again repeated his examination of the street and alcove as he read the police reports aloud.

'Anne Chapman, a lady of ill repute, was last seen alive at 5:30 AM on the morning of September 8.' Holmes moved about catlike dramatically continuing his graphic description of the victim. *'She was strangled, slashed across her face and disemboweled just like the first victim, Polly Ann Nichols.*

'On her body were only several meager possessions; a small comb, a paper case where the killer had laid two brass rings at her feet. Near her head was part of an envelope and a piece of paper containing two pills - on the back of the envelope was the postal seal of the Sussex Regiment and on the other the letter M with a postmark dated 28 Aug. 1888.'

The cheap brass rings seemed to occupy Holmes thoughts. "Ah, the rings, Gentlemen. Again the curious rings. What do you make of it, Watson … Inspector?"

"Well, Holmes", I stammered, not quite prepared for the query. "The rings would most likely be cheap jewelry or a gift from one of her men friends."

Holmes turned to The Inspector. "I agree with Dr. Watson; inexpensive costume jewelry ... from a man friend."

"Yes! I would agree with you both ... a man friend. But not a client, rather a provider, or protector ... a manager of sorts. I believe the ladies of the night refer to them as their Johnny Boys and the brass rings are a mark of indentured servitude instead of a disfiguring firebrand."

The Inspector seemed very interested at this new possibility ... as he spoke. "Yes, I would agree that would make sense. These Johnny Boys are a cruel lot ... tough masters, quick with a razor or knife, to keep a girl in her place, and known to mark their property. We did question some of them, but nothing came of it."

"I would have guessed that. It would be too obvious to point the finger at the Johnny Boy. However, Watson, that will be our next step in the investigation; questing out the last two victims' Johnny Boys."

"Be careful, Mr. Holmes. As I said, they're a tough lot, quick with the blade and do not take kindly to being questioned."

As we investigated the last two murder scenes (the double event), Holmes seemed to become less interested with each location. Perhaps he had reached a conclusion about the murders.

That evening back in our digs, we enjoyed a hot cup of tea and a hearty meal of beef prepared by Mrs. Hudson. I took to reading the latest medical journal, as was my custom, while Holmes worked with his chemicals and reference books.

The large board was a mass of notes and diagrams, making sense only to their designer. I looked at it several times, finding it all too confusing, and returned to my books and pipe, for the what was to become an all too brief respite from the case.

We ran, striking several men as we burst into the welcoming
London fog among shouts of 'Ripper!' 'Leather apron!'
'Butcher!'

CHAPTER 4

BIRDS AND JACKALS

Over the next few days Holmes worked relentlessly on the case files, going back and forth to that small room at Scotland Yard, and resting only to nibble on a bit of food or sip a cup of tea. His untidy appearance and unshaven face gave him the look of a derelict, an appearance I was to find out was exactly what he wanted. I would, only with the greatest reluctance, agree to see a patient in my room, preferring to spare any visitors the unkempt sight of the great detective.

Late that night he jumped up from his chair, bursting with new found energy, causing me to awake with a start from a drowsy nap in my reading chair. "Come, Watson. The game is afoot and we must join in the chase."

As the fog of sleep lifted from my eyes I began to see more clearly ... a stranger standing before me, an East End ruffian type, unshaved with a scar running across his brow to his ear. It was Holmes, of course, dressed in another of his numerous disguises about which I could write a separate book. The particular style of dress suggested to me a Johnny Boy type ... tattoos ... earring ... ring and knife.

I knew his methods and knew what was expected. He threw a tattered cape to me which would hide my well-tailored

clothing and keep out the damp chill of the London fog ...
which was quite dense as we left for the Bower Street area
of Whitechapel ...

We arrived by carriage just on the outskirts. Holmes paid
the driver, telling him where to wait for what may be an
extended period of time. The driver knew Holmes and
could be trusted to follow instructions. We moved
cautiously through the fog ... barely making out the
shadows of passing people.

"Watson," Holmes whispered, "You will address me only
as Jack Crow ... and speak only when I ask you to. I will
address you as Doc, a shady abortionist."

"Holmes, really, I would appreciate your asking my opinion
about my part in this ... play acting. It's an intolerable
thought to think that I ..."

Holmes interrupted. "Be a good fellow and go along. We
have a much too important charge, and, as you say, it is
only play acting; but keep your revolver handy."

I submitted, of course. He was right. The capture of this
fiend of the night took precedence over our personal egos.
I did not know the location to which Holmes was taking
us, but I was sure it would be a pub frequented by the ladies
of the night, their customers, and of course, their Johnny
Boys.

We would have to be very cautious ... not only of the ruffian
types but of the ladies as well who have been reported to
give a good accounting of themselves in a fight. Razors in
their stockings could cut a man to ribbons.

And, of course, there was the "Ripper", too. Suppose we
were to come across his path in the fog?!!!   These
unnerving thoughts accompanied me until we stopped in

front of a dimly lit hanging sign with the drawing of a lion's head and the words "Lion's Den".

How appropriate! I thought of the biblical Daniel as well as ourselves as we entered. The smoke was thicker than the fog outside. It was a crowded pub filled with sounds of gregarious laughter of the ladies and their drinking partners.

Somewhere in a dark corner men threw darts at a hanging board as a happy tune sounded from a small accordion instrument. We could make out some of the 'Ripper' conversation taking place as we passed the tables looking for a place to sit. We found one uncomfortably near the dart board wall as a large shirt-sleeved waiter approached, looking us over. "What'll it be, Mates? Devil's rum?...a pint?"

Holmes replied in his best cockney, "A pint 'n a bit of the Devil for me mate." The waiter stood silent, glaring at us both as he leaned forward, wiping the dirty candle-lit table with an even dirtier rag.

"'Ere ... I've never seen you two in here b'fore." He parted his lips, gritting his tobacco-stained teeth as he awaited our answer.

Holmes looked back at him just as menacingly with his hand on the knife handle in his belt. "What's it to you? We're not coppers!   ... just in from the docks ... looking for a few birds that I might want to set up a nest with ... and a little something in it for you if you can help." Smiling, Holmes threw a couple of coppers and a golden sovereign on the table.

The leering waiter smiled and stood upright as he said, "I'll take the money now and talk to a bird or two. I wouldn't expect you to be around later for me to collect what you owe me when their Johnny Boys find out!

With that he left, laughing as we watched him go back to the bar whispering into the ears of two ladies. One of the ladies looked over smiling. She started to approach our table: the younger one followed. Holmes, wearing a lecherous look, of course, was quite convincing.

I started to rise, but Holmes kicked my shin. The ladies seated themselves. The younger one, dressed in blue; the much older one in gaudy red beads and heavy makeup. Youth needs little window dressing while age needs numerous accessories to compensate for the unmerciful ravages of time.

The older one spoke first. "'ello, Gov'ner. Looking for a hot time on a cold night? Barney," she crocked her head back toward the bar, "says you 'ave a business proposition to offer a couple of birds. My name's Kitty, and this 'ere is Sally."

Sally smiled, saying nothing. Evidently they were partners; the older being more experienced, ran the show, with the younger being attractive, ... attracting the bees to the honey and, if necessary, to the Queen Bee herself.

Holmes started looking them over as he nudged me to join in smiling, too. "Well, we got ourselves a couple of pretty birds and we ain't been in the joint more than a few minutes. What da ya say to that, Doc?" He leaned toward me.

I smiled uncomfortably back, nodding my head. Holmes continued to leer and laugh as Barney returned with our drinks and two for the ladies. "Thanks, Barney!" she said. "'E always knows what we like to drink." Holmes threw Barney some more coins and that just made the women laugh even louder as the younger one, turning to me, spoke for the first time. "Are you a real doctor, Doc?" she giggled.

I started to speak, looking for Holmes to rescue me from the questions ... which he did in an instant. "A real doctor, 'E is, and a good one at that; especially if you ladies need a little 'elp ... getting rid of a bellyache." He smiled that lecherous smile even broader as he leaned over the table toward the ladies. "If you know what I mean," as he elbowed the older woman in the ribs.

She laughed a guffaw as she nodded back, "'Deed I do, Dearie. 'Deed I do!"

The smile faded from Holmes face as he took on a more serious tone with the women. "You ladies want to talk some real business ... I mean big money business.?"

The older one leaned back taking Holmes hand in hers as she answered. "That depends on what you call big, Dearie." We all laughed some more.

"Jack ... Jack Crow ... call me Jack, Kitty."

"All right, Jack. What's your proposition 'n it betta be good ... and you betta be good with 'at knife yer warren in that belt if you expect us to cross over from Jimmy, our Johnny Boy."

Holmes took her hands, examining the fingers in particular. "Don't worry about your Jimmy. I'll see to that. Is 'E the one that makes the birds wear them cheap brass rings?" Her face drained white, her eyes widened.

The younger woman's mouth dropped open. She struggled to speak ... saying, "No! No! That would be Alfie's girls. ... the dead ones." She hoisted up her drink, draining the glass in one gulp. "The Ripper got 'um! We don't wear no rings. But Kelly does. She's one of Alfie's girls."

"Shut up," snapped Kitty, "Jimmy will hear."

Just as she was about to drink again, the whizzing sound of a dart struck our table, just between the fingers of Holmes right hand...We all sat back, ridged and upright, as three men approached the table from the Dart Board game.

The one man leading the other two ruffian types came forward, throwing more darts into the table as emphasis for each sentence. "These 'ere birds belong to me, Mate." The girls stood up. "I don't like anyone feeding my birds but mee ... see!" as another dart struck the table, this time our hands were at our sides.

"Jimmy, we waz just talkin' business, 'ats all. We thought 'E was a customer." Jimmy turned and slapped her across her mouth as he pulled back the younger one, throwing her to the floor.

Holmes and I jumped up as I started to shout, "How dare you, Sir, treat these women in that manner. You should be taken out and horsewhipped."

Homes stopped me from continuing further as I realized I was out of character. "Hold it, Doc. 'Es just taking care of business. I understand. No 'arm done. We'll be leavin'. C'mon, Doc."

"Oh, a doctor, is 'E!" he sneered and threw a dart as his men moved closer. "A doctor with a black bag, too. Let's 'ave a look inside and see ya bloody knives!"

"I have no bag, Sir." I shouted as we slowly backed out toward the door. I hid my bag behind my back.

The women started to move toward us, too, as Kitty began to join in what can only be described as a stalking pack of hungry jackals preparing to attack and bring down the prey.

"'Ats right, Jimmy, the papers say leather apron ... might be a doctor ... and these two were asking about Alfie's girls. 'E could be the Ripper!" sneered Kitty.

The men reacted to Kitty's words with even more rage as they neared the bursting point. ... attack was eminent. "You'll be leavin' all right. You're gonna need this fancy Doc to stitch you up when we get through with you!" With that he pulled a large dagger type knife from beneath his coat, coming at Holmes, who stood his ground and quite easily tumbled the fellow over the table and into a brick wall using his far eastern method of fighting which he had studied for some time.

The other two stopped dead in their tracks as I put my revolver into their faces. A flying knife struck the wall behind us. Holmes threw over a table into their path and I fired two shots into the ceiling bringing down plaster amongst the gunsmoke. It was sufficient to startle and confuse the snarling pack. We ran, striking several men as we burst into the welcoming London fog among shouts of 'Ripper!' 'Leather apron!' 'Butcher!' We could hear the sounds of their running fect on the cobblestones as we hid in a side alley. The sounds diminished into silence and we cautiously made our way back to our waiting carriage driver.

We reviewed the events of the evening episode as we rode home to Baker Street. "Holmes, that was an excellent display of ... ... what do you call that eastern art of fighting?"

"Jitsu, an ancient form of far eastern fighting. The principal concept being to use your opponents own force of movement to overcome him. ... That's not important. We have the name of our Johnny Boy, the one with the brass rings. He is the key to this bad business."

"The Ripper?" I asked.

"No, merely the catalytic agent." Holmes was jubilant, having succeeded in his mission. He was content to work further on the puzzle mounted on his evidence board, while I was more interested in continuing my reading, and a nap.

"... Gentlemen. Brace yourselves for the worst. I am still unsettled by it. I have seen many a mess when it comes to dead bodies, but never, never ..." His words faded from his mouth as we started to enter the room.

CHAPTER 5

THE NEXT VICTIM

That next afternoon we sought out the Johnny Boy who Holmes believed would lead us to the killer or killers. We were careful not be draw too much attention to ourselves down at the docks, where he was reported to live. This information was obtained through police reports of the murder victims.

Alfie had been questioned and released as there was no direct evidence connecting him to the crimes, and he had accounted for his movements on the murder nights.

Alibis were easy to come by in Whitechapel, but Holmes believed it unlikely that the rouge types of Whitechapel would provide an alibi for the brutal murder of one of their own. There was a limit even to their allegiance to each other. Their code of conduct, while baffling to law abiding citizens, never the less, was understandable to them ... perhaps even necessary for their own survival. Those less fortunate rabble had to close ranks against the outside upper class.

Holmes wanted to find the woman, Jeanette Marie Kelly, believing her to be the next target of the Ripper.

We found Alfie's digs in a rear ground floor apartment of an old waterfront warehouse. After making our way through a mound of storage debris and rat infested garbage, we saw a door. It was ajar just enough to peer in and see a snoring body sprawled across a small cot. Apparently sleeping off the drinking episode of the previous night. This was obvious to the eye by viewing the empty bottle half-filled with whiskey, a glass and the smell of bar liquor.

The man slowly sat up, having become aware of our presence. It was late afternoon and perhaps he was arousing himself for the night's work. He rubbed his eyes and scratched himself as he said, "'Ere! What you gentlemen want? If it's a bird, you're a bit early. Come back in two hours."

"It's not any woman we want, just a particular one. ... a Jeanette Kelly." The mention of her name electrified him to jump up. His eyes widened, and he looked at us suspiciously.

"If yer the coppers, I already told 'em about Jeanette Kelly. If yer not, than I'll tell you what I tol' them. I dunno where she is. 'aven't seen her since my last two birds were slaughtered by that Bastard Ripper."

"We are not the police." Holmes replied. "We are investigating the murders and trying to stop this insane slaughter of your women. That should be in your best interest as well.

Could these murders have been committed by one of your competitors?" I blurted out.

"Naw, they wouldn't kill the birds. They would steal 'em away by paying a few quid more. ... And besides they was nuttin' special about 'em. They're not like Kelly. She was a real beauty. But I guess this Ripper business scared her off and she already has enough trouble."

"What trouble?" Holmes asked.

"Well, I suppose it's O.K. to tell you gentlemen, but a few quid would 'elp me get back on my feet. Since I lost the birds I ain't been doing so good ya know."

Holmes walked over to the bed, lifting it upward from the floor, making visible the items beneath. "Is that why you have three full bottles of whiskey, a night bag packed for a trip, and some sovereigns which I hear jingling in your pockets?"

His cocky expression changed to uncertainty and what might have been fear as he stuttered. "Well, … I … well … I been sick. I 'ave to go to the country. This business ain't healthy."

Holmes dropped the bed loudly to the floor as he took Alfie by the shoulders. "You arranged the meeting for these women and they were brutally murdered. You may have fooled the police but I doubt your friends in Whitechapel will be so sympathetic to your downturn in business when they find out you were the Judas Goat leading the ladies to slaughter."

With that, Alfie bolted for the doorway, but I was quick enough to close the door and he was unable to stop his running momentum and ran into it.

"Excellent, Watson!" Holmes shouted as he leaned over the man, now on his knees and regaining his wits from the door encounter.

"I didn't know! I didn't know he was goin' to do 'em that way. I thought the first was another blither who got 'er afterward. But after the second one, I knew. ... I tried to stop ... but 'E said 'E would do the same to me 'n more if I talked to anyone."

"His name ? ... His description! It's your only hope for safety. Tell us now."

"'E never gave me is name. He just told me what to do and when. ... "

"Did he ask for those particular women?"

"Yes! Yes! 'E made sure it was these birds. 'E gave me money and said to leave London last night, but I got drunk. Please let me go! 'E said 'e would kill me if I stayed.

"What did he look like?"

"Big like a bear, 'E was ... had a mustache and scar on 'E's face/"

"A scar!" Holmes shouted as if stuck with a pin. "Was it running from his left ear to across his throat?"

"Yes! Yes! 'ats 'em!! Please, Gov'ner, I got to get out." He was sweating profusely, breathing heavy, and ... as Holmes grabbed him by the collar...

"Where is Jeanette Kelly and what trouble was she in.?"

The struggling Alfie couldn't get the words out fast enough to Holmes as he was anxious to make his getaway. "She said she 'ad trouble in Ireland ... turned in a rebel boyfriend to the Army for money ... and said they would come to kill her if they could find her. She only worked a few weeks. Enough to get some money and leave the country. ... I tol' the big man she left last night and 'E left. 'E was mad as 'ell ... foaming at the mouth, he was."

"Where is Kelly? ... Where is the woman?" Holmes continued to hold the babbling fool by the collar when a shot rang out, barely missing Holmes' shoulder, but finding its mark in Alfie's head between the eyes.

Holmes dropped the man who fell like a bundle of wet rags to the cold floor. I fired my revolver several times indiscriminately in the direction of the shot as we both dropped behind a box and chair.

"Wait, Watson! Listen!" We could hear the sound of running feet. We followed the running sound into the dark warehouse, not knowing exactly which direction the killer was running. Several more shots were fired by the killer and I returned fire in the direction of the gun flashes. ... And then, silence. The only sound we could hear was our own breathing and beating hearts. We moved, spreading out slowly. Holmes with his sword cane which he had removed from its sheath, and I with an empty gun ...

Suddenly a large number of bales filled with soft goods was tumbling on top of us, pinning my legs so that I was unable to stand to meet the running silhouette of a large man coming toward us waving a sword. Holmes met the onslaught with a skillful report of his own sword.

I was unable to assist Holmes in the fight. I had no more bullets. I tried desperately to extricate myself from the large bale pinning my legs while Homes exchanged clashing blades, sparking in the dark. The two men grunted as they exchanged blows. I heard Holmes reply, "Me thinks your blade a bit dull for this job, Dearie." A pun, to taunt the killer no doubt, and to distract his concentration.

For a moment I thought he had Holmes, but then again it was difficult to make out Holmes in the darkness. More bales were overturned and the killer ran away, preferring, no doubt, a more advantageous contact at another time and place.

Homes did not continue the chase out of concern for me as he was not certain if I was critically injured by the falling bales. I assured him I was fit to continue, but Holmes believed the culprit had succeeded in alluding us for the moment.

"Come, we must find the Kelly woman before the colonel does."

"The colonel?" I interrupted. "You know his identity?"

"Yes. The scar was the confirmation I needed. His likeness is amongst my file of criminal sketches. He received the scar from a tiger attack in India, and ... I know more than that, Watson. Much more."

Late that night found us in the heavy London fog of Whitechapel outside the Lion's Den Pub. Not wanting to repeat the incident of our previous excursion into the area I left my doctor's bag at home and Holmes did not wear a disguise.

We found ourselves a darkened corner and waited until daybreak for Kitty or young Sally to appear. Luck was with us as a drunken' sailor appeared under the gas lighted street lamp with Sally holding him up after what must have been a satisfactory sexual liaison. He dropped to a sitting position as Holmes moved out to intercept her path to the Lion's Den Pub.

"Could you spare a moment for a lonely man, Sally?" She was obviously a little less cautious due to the drinking I suppose, because she smiled, moving forward to Holmes.

"Sure, Honey. Say? 'ow cum ya know my name? 'ave I been with ya before?" she giggled.

Holmes pulled her by the arm, swiftly clasping his hand over her mouth as he dragged her into the alcove. She was horrified! No doubt, believing it was the Ripper. Her widened eyes filled with fear and dread as Holmes, holding her tightly, said, "I am not the Ripper. We are not going to hurt you. You must not scream. We want to stop the killings and we need your help to do it. Will you help us?"

The girl, relieved that she was not to be put upon the butcher's block almost fainted, but shook her head, 'Yes', as Holmes slowly removed his hand from her pouting lips. She stifled a tearful cry and began to wipe away a tear. "How can I 'elp, Sir, I'm jus' a street girl? Her petite frame wobbled a bit as both Holmes and I held her steady.

Homes, looking directly into her eyes with a forceful glare, spoke, "Where is Jeanette Kelly? Where does she live? Tell us and you will be rewarded and put safe from the Ripper."

The girl, still terrified but feeling safe, responded, "I know she lives near the Christ Church near Millers Court. She never said where exactly ... like she was 'iding from somebody. Can I leave, now? My Johnny Boy will beat me if I'm late with the money."

We were both saddened to see this pretty little flower begin to wilt so early in her chosen wretched life. We let her go with a warning to say nothing to her Johnny Boy or anyone else as it might endanger her safety. Holmes was sure she would obey.

Our carriage rode through the dense fog, slowing from time to time as the driver attempted to find his way to the Christ Church. Holmes, however, was impatient in his race against death, and rapped his cane against the carriage ceiling, yelling to the driver, "Hurry!!"...

I could restrain myself no longer. "Holmes, who is the colonel??"

"He is a very dangerous man ... more a beast than a man. He started to continue as we approached Christ Church, but stopped as we heard the sound of Bobby whistles and shouts of 'The Ripper! The Ripper!'

We quickly dismounted from the carriage as Holmes shouted back at me. "Come, Watson! I fear we are too late."

We followed the running Bobbies through several streets, past Millers Court to Bushfield Street where several other Bobbies had roped off the entrance to a small gray brick building. We could see through a dirty window several uniformed men inside the small dimly lit room. We approached the Sergeant who seemed to be in charge. I identified Homes and myself.

"Sorry, Sir, You'll have to wait here while I get the Chief Inspector."

We watched him walk to the inside of the entrance and stood by impatiently as Holmes, ever the detective, scrutinized whatever area he could examine from our vantage point.

The Inspector came out of the building and hurriedly directed the Sergeant to let us pass, waving us forward to the front of the building. The wet streets were reflecting the figures in the window, but not the unspeakable horror inside. The Inspector stopped our progress as he spoke. "How did you know about this murder, Mr. Holmes? The body was only found this morning, within the past 1/2 hour."

"Is it Kelly?" Holmes asked.

"Marie Jeanette! How do you know who lives here? We just found out that information from papers inside ... and the neighbors ... "

"That is of no importance. Now, may we enter and see the body?"

"Frankly, Mr. Holmes, I'm not sure of anything. Least of all the body, if that's what it can be called. The Inspector paused, taking a deep breath, as he wiped his brow. It's a terrible sight, Gentlemen. Brace yourselves for the worst. I am still unsettled by it. I have seen many a mess when it comes to dead bodies, but never, never ..." His words faded from his mouth as we started to enter the room.

While thankful for his efforts to prepare us for the ungodly sight we were to view, I can honestly say, there was nothing that could prepare us for this work of the Devil. The other men in the room were turning away from the sight. Still others were pale with illness.

Having treated war wounded and walked among the dead remnants of soldier bodies, I was still shocked, but less unnerved, than was Holmes who, upon viewing the sight of the butchered woman on the bed, very nearly fainted.

His knees buckled as he grabbed my arm for support saying, "My God, Watson. This is far too much to burn into a sane man's brain." She or what could be referred to as 'it', a vacant discarded carcass, was reduced in part to a near skeleton by the removal of flesh, organs, and other body parts lying on a table beside the bed. I will not further describe the horror of it all except to say the smell of blood and the sight of it covered the entire room.

I decided it best to assist Holmes from the room into the morning air, thankful for its damp wetness which seemed to offer a cleansing of sorts. I lit a pipe as Holmes, having some difficulty with his shaking hands, lit a cigarette. We did not speak for a long moment, letting the shock wear a little thinner until finally he spoke.

"Watson ... if I appeared emotionally detached from the murders before this night, I can say to you now, this case is more than just another stimulating adventure. It has become a quest. I vow to capture this fiend and see that he receives his earthly punishment before he stands in front of his maker for the eternal damnation of his soul."

The Inspector came from the building taking deep breaths as he spoke. "Mr. Holmes, is there anything you care to tell us?"

"Yes. I will keep you informed by letter as Watson and I must leave London tonight to continue our investigations. But be assured I will not rest until the fiend is brought to justice."

"Have you determined the time of the murder?" Holmes asked.

"It is difficult to tell from the condition of the body, but someone heard a woman scream, 'Oh, Murder!' ..." at about 4 AM.

Glad to have left the murder scene, we arrived back at Baker Street where upon Holmes enlightened me further about the colonel and the unsettling details of his investigations as he gathered his notes from his Case Board.

"We have him now, Watson. I know who he is and where he is, but I don't know the why. And until I do, we are powerless to act."

"But how can we not act. He may murder again ... tonight perhaps."

"Yes, I know. But the greater gain must outweigh the small loss. I not only knew he was going to strike tonight, but who he was to strike, and that is why I tried to save her. In Switzerland two years ago there were a series of "Ripper-type" murders ... five victims. In Paris last year ... five. So far here in London, ... five.. If I'm not mistaken., the killings are over. If we act too soon, we may do a greater harm. Only one mindless creature could perpetuate such monstrous violence for a purpose... and he is the heir to the Throne of Satan."

"Moriarty!!!??"

"Exactly! Him! The evil force behind a thousand misdeeds; the Napoleon of Crime. I must know his purpose. He has the entire city in a panic. The government is about to topple, ...riots in the streets. The full resources of the Scotland Yard chasing a shadow... Wait, wait! That's it! A diversion! He has created this diversion here while he moves about elsewhere. There were so many clues. Too many. They were obvious distractions... of that much I was sure."

"But how do you know it's Moriarty?"

"Because that madman can't resist putting his signature to the crime. He is an artist who, having blended his paints upon the canvas to his satisfaction, needs only to apply the

final touch - his mark of "the creator"!" Holmes explained
the letters sent by the "Ripper" gave many clues of the
streets and victims, and formed Moriarty's abstract
signature, which was designed to confuse and torment
Scotland Yard Investigators.

He took me by the arm, standing me before his clue board,
then released his grip to explain further. "Look, here,
Watson, I have an exact copy of the official city map of the
Whitechapel area marked with the locations where each
of the 4 victims' bodies were found. — Moriarty has
already signed his work."

"How can you determine his mark? I see no obvious clues,
but I have no doubt they are there."

"Oh, but they are there! Now, observe. I draw straight
lines connecting each of the victims ... 1 - 2 ... 3 - 4. We
now see what appears to be 2 perfect geometric triangles
of which the length and distance of each is almost exactly
the same."

"Yes, I see, but what does it mean?"

"It means, my dear fellow, that Moriarty, a genius at
mathematics is sending us a message. The triangle is a
mathematical symbol of the pyramids which are themselves
a wonder of mathematics. They are aligned true north;
they are precisely leveled and constructed so as to confound
even modern engineering technology; and they are solar
observatories that can calculate the exact periods of the
solar equinox and much more — They are a storehouse of
mathematics, and that is Moriarty's signature. See how
the lines of the triangle form a symbolic 'M'?

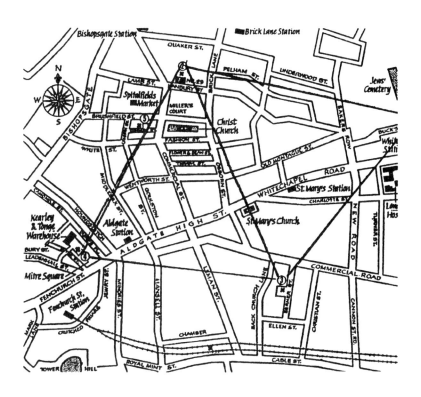

Murder Locations of

Jack the Ripper

"See ... here, copies of letters sent to the police?" He pointed to the letters mounted on his board. "See, Watson, ... signed by 2 seemingly different signatures. Yet they are identical. The difference in the writing angles is achieved by changing the position of the paper. And each victim attended the same London medical clinic for the poor."

"But if that is so, Holmes, then you were right. The killings were not random; they had to be planned."

"Precisely. Each woman was marked for death beforehand. Come, Watson, we leave tonight for the continent. There is a lady in Paris who wishes to tell us much more, ... and pack for an extended trip. We go on to Switzerland from there; I have him and his organization in my sights."

"He is not alone in this?"

"No. His organization pervades the whole of Europe, and his Chief Second in Command, is none other than the infamous Colonel Sebastian Moran, a bull of a man who is both fearless and a natural survivalist; he has written books on the subject. He once tracked a wounded man-eating tiger down into its lair. Cashiered from the service, he now works for the highest bidder as a mercenary. He is a determined foe and we must be cautious. Our last encounter with the Colonel was almost fatal."

Satisfied we were not followed, we took the night boat train from Victoria Station on that chilly November night and I confess a dreaded feeling of foreboding accompanied us as I felt that for the first time Holmes was experiencing fear.

I had been no stranger to the feeling and during several military skirmishes had tasted the dry morsel of near death.

No words passed between us during the train trip. None were necessary.

The next few days proved me right about my feelings of unrest, but a new development awaited us in Paris that proved to be both vital to the case and extraordinarily unsettling to Holmes.

"How convenient to have you both here. Now put down the blade, and give me the gun, Dr. Watson, or I'll put a bloody smile on the lady's throat."

CHAPTER 6

THE LADY IN PARIS

A Madame Fontaine of Paris had written a letter to Holmes requesting an urgent meeting as she has information of great importance concerning the Ripper murders.

When I asked Holmes if he knew the nature of information, he said, "If it concurs with the data I have compiled, it may well solve the case. We are to meet the lady at an out-of-the-way coffee house on the Left Bank. She advises caution as she fears she may be followed."

Upon leaving the station, Holmes, as was his custom, selected, not the first or even the second or third cabby, but the fourth, much to the consternation of the first carriage driver. We drove around the city for several hours as our meeting with Madame Fontaine would be in the early evening. We changed carriages several times and finally selected an obscure, but presentable, hotel to change from our travel clothes and refresh ourselves with dinner.

At 8 o'clock that eve Holmes gave the driver his instructions in his best French, but the driver was accustomed to the tourist from England and fared far better with his English than we did with our French.

We arrived at the coffee house and walked through the outside street tables crowded with the local group of artists, more interested in the philosophy of life than the day to day reality. There were several people with charcoal and paper ... a sculptor working on a small block of marble ... poets ... and two dancers whose movements applied themselves to the sounds of a roving accordionist.

We saw no women fitting the description Madame Fontaine had given Holmes; a redheaded lady with light complexion, green eyes, wearing a black hat containing an outcropping of two small red birds. We continued our search inside the coffee house, going down an uneven stone stairway into the cellar of the coffee house. It was dimly lit and smoke filled air made it difficult to see the faces of the people sitting at the small cheesecloth tables sipping coffee and wine.

What appeared to be a small stage rose up in the corner of the room, obviously used by the artists and poets to display their work. Thankfully, it was empty at the moment, giving us the opportunity to find Madame Fontaine at a nearby table without attracting attention to ourselves. She was as she described herself, in every detail; hair, skin, and eye colors; ... only modestly omitting her own beauty. Not sure of our identity she gave us a short side glance and the smallest movement of one finger from her clasped hands on the table top.

We approached her, removing our hats as Holmes spoke in an almost inaudible whisper. "Madame Fontaine, I am Sherlock Holmes and this is my friend and associate, Dr. Watson."

She smiled and beckoned us to seat ourselves with the movement of her eyes. We did so and for a brief moment none of us spoke. I decided to break the strained silence. "May we order some tea or coffee, as I notice you have not ordered as of yet?!"

"Yes, thank you, Dr. Watson."

"It is very fortuitous that you have brought Dr. Watson with you, Mr. Holmes."

Holmes replied, "The good doctor's assistance has been invaluable to me on many occasions and I believe this instance will be the same, but why do you make that observation?"

"Because, Mr. Holmes, if my plan meets with your approval; our success may depend on the doctor's skillful knowledge of the strange experiments taking place at the clinic where I do volunteer work."

"Does the nature of these experiments have to do with the information you wish to entrust to me."

"It does!" she replied in an authoritative tone.

Holmes seemed to glow with the excitement of new clues to be added to his stew. "Madame Fontaine, I believe as you do, that the Ripper murders of London somehow relate to a series of similar murders … incidents in Paris last year.

"If your information can enlighten me further, I would be most grateful, as would the police of Scotland Yard. This business must be finished as soon as possible for all concerned. Tell us. How did you come to be the source of this information? I know of your late husband's philanthropic activities and his untimely death several years ago. I assume you are carrying on his work in his place and that is how you came to be doing social work at the clinic. You are fluent in French and English; you were born in Scotland and educated in England and France."

She was impressed with the details Holmes had uncovered about her husband and replied, "Why, yes, Mr. Holmes. You are quite correct. My late husband, Andrea, died suddenly of ill health, but he provided for me very generously so that I would never be destitute. We have no children and I am still young and energetic enough to help the less fortunate. Andrea would have wanted me to continue his work. I had been working at the Paris clinic these ..."

At that moment a waiter interrupted us to put four coffees, four glasses and a bottle of red wine on the table, while presenting us with a bill. I tossed some money on the table which seemed to satisfy him and after lighting another candle on the table he promptly left.

Madame Fontaine waited until he was out of earshot before continuing. "I have been counseling several women ... patients." She paused, too embarrassed to say the words, but we spared her the need to say the word, as she continued, overcoming her embarrassment. "These women, all in trouble by men, came to the clinic seeking assistance. I do not condone interrupting the life of a child to be nor does the clinic. We offer medical and financial assistance only. At least that's what I was led to believe when I volunteered for the work.

"After reading about the deaths of the first two Ripper victims in London, I remembered their faces from the newspaper drawings, in the London paper, a copy of which I accidentally saw in the administrative office at the clinic. These women came here by way of a Placur, a French name for a recruiter of women for pleasure." Madame Fontaine lowered her head in embarrassment as she continued.

"When the women were in trouble they were referred to the clinic for assistance and then given passage money back to England. I do not know the full extent of the clinic's involvement with the women and the Placurs, but there must be a connection, so I thought it best to contact you discreetly and meet with you secretly so that your investigation would not be encumbered in any way.

I have, on occasion, raised money to assist the clinic financially by soliciting wealthy acquaintances and charitable organizations. I propose that I present you and Dr. Watson, with fictitious names of course, to the clinic Administrators as Board Members of a charitable English Trust investigating worthy organizations to contribute to financially. They will not refuse to see you on that basis if I tell them you are only in Paris for one day.

"Yes. That is an excellent plan and we must prepare our play for presentation tomorrow." Holmes said. His mood was elevated by the prospect of another exciting encounter with suspects.

As we concluded the details of our play, the roaming accordion player followed by the male and female dancers moved about the tables; he with a cigarette hanging limply from his rugged unshaven face and her with a red ribbon around her throat. She wore an immodest tight shirt exposing a heaving and bounteous full bosom. Her dress was short with a slit down one side revealing a shapely leg encased in a smoky silk stocking.

The sight was comfortably unsettling to me as it would be to any healthy man. But Holmes seemed engrossed in his thoughts and the charms of Madame Fontaine.

The dancers moved quickly about performing some sort of sexual ritual involving her slapping him and him retaliating with a slap to her face which almost brought me to my feet, but Holmes and Madame Fontaine restrained my act of gallantry, advising that it was all part of an entertainment ruse customarily performed in these coffee houses.

I re-seated myself somewhat uncomfortably as the dancers continued to dance to what sounded like a new form of Spanish dance now pervading the European countries. He threw the woman to the floor. She grabbed his leg as he tried to walk away. He slapped her arms as she folded her head into her bent legs. Suddenly she leapt up with a small dagger in her hand, running at the male dancer whose back was now turned away.

Once again I felt compelled to intercede, but Holmes' reassuring glances bade me to restrain myself.

The male dancer turned in time to stop the downward thrust of the dagger, grabbing her wrist and then gripping her tightly around her small waist, forcing her body up against his. Their faces were inches apart ... when she surrendered the knife first and then herself to his embrace as they kissed passionately.

Quite suddenly the room roared with cheers and applause. We all joined in. It seemed out of place for the moment, but was a welcome respite from the ghastly business at hand.

As we continued talking about the meeting tomorrow, the male dancer strode over to our table and leaning over between our heads he flatly placed two palms on the table looking into Madame Fontaine's face, separated only by a few inches from his own. He was speaking to her in French, but we could make out enough of what he said to Madame Fontaine to know he was being crude and asking her to dance with him as the accordionist and the female dancer waited off to the side.

Madame Fontaine was beside herself and nervously attempted to graciously avoid and withdraw from what could be a difficult and dangerous situation. Suddenly the man reached over, pulling Madame Fontaine to her feet as both Holmes and I leapt from our chairs.

Holmes was closer and quicker, grabbing the man's hand he twisted it, bringing the man to his knees and then shoved him backwards over a chair. Two of his ruffian friends helped him to his feet. He held out a knife as Holmes grabbed Madame Fontaine and slapped her across the face.

I stood gaping with shock at Holmes' actions. The man stood back, holding the knife to his side as Holmes pulled Madame Fontaine into an embrace, kissing her and then dancing out into the room to the accompaniment of the accordionist, who continued to play throughout the entire incident.

The female dancer went up to her man, leaning against his body, as they both smiled approvingly of Holmes' actions, as did the rest of the coffee house crowd. This, after all, was Paris!

Holmes and Madame Fontaine danced with surprising agility and accomplishment. There was no need for me to ask Holmes about this unknown talent of his as he would only say it was geometrically simple. I had long ago learned to understand his motives and actions, no matter how insane they seemed at the moment. To the French this was normal and romantic.

We left shortly thereafter, not divulging to Madame Fontaine where we were staying for secrecy was imperative. We agreed to meet at the clinic the next midday and then we parted, but not before Holmes offered his earnest apology for the slapping and kissing incident.

She smiled and simply put Holmes off his guard by saying, "No apology is necessary. You saved us all from a most unpleasant situation by inventing a most pleasurable one."

She half-closed those shiny green eyes leaving us both staring speechless in the Paris rain as we watched her carriage speed away.

The next morning Holmes posted more letters to Scotland Yard. And after a hearty breakfast we departed for the clinic to begin our play. The clinic was situated just outside Paris along the riverbank and tucked between two small rolling hills. It was pleasant to look at and absent of the dreary gray brick color of the clinics that pervaded the London slums. To the contrary it appeared more as a country school or estate; flowing gardens and twisted shrubs; two pathways were bordered by fountains on either side.

The sight of it all seemed to relax much of my tension, but Holmes managed to snap me back to the reality of the situation by saying, "The spider's web is most attractive."

We approached the front doors as Madame Fontaine shouted out a loud greeting; no doubt for effect. "Mr. Sacker ... Dr. Blair. Won't you come in!?"

We entered a lavishly furnished foyer and hallway; velvet drapes, mahogany wood trim, and leather couches ... tables covered with plants and fresh flowers ... honey to the bee. We removed our coats and hats. Holmes retained his cane feigning a slight limp while I kept my loaded revolver in my hip pocket. We greeted her according to our scripted play and followed her to the Chief Administrator's office where we were presented to Dr. Ormon, an elderly, but seemingly robust man of 70.

"Ah, Mr. Sacker and Dr. Blair. How good of you to come. I understand you are pressed for time and can only visit us for a short while."

Holmes replied, "Yes, but charity is our charge and first priority and we will take the time necessary, Dr. Ormon, to offer a worthy organization our financial assistance."

"Well, then, suppose I conduct a tour of our facility as I take a personal pride in our accomplishments, which I am sure you, Dr. Blair, can appreciate from a medical standpoint."

I replied that I was sure there was much to interest me from a medical standpoint, but little that would be appreciated by a non-medical person such as my associate, Mr. Sacker. I suggested that he be given a separate tour, perhaps by Madame Fontaine who could present the non-medical perspective of the clinic.

"Yes, of course. Excellent, Dr. Madame Fontaine, would you mind showing Mr. Sacker our facilities' patient rooms, library, exercise room, and such? I will return within the hour and perhaps we can all have lunch in the dining room."

"I would be delighted!" said Madame Fontaine, as I followed Dr. Ormon into the medical laboratory.

I was to learn later what discoveries Holmes had uncovered as I conducted my own investigation. I was escorted into what appeared to be a small research facility as the doctor explained its purpose.

"We are attempting to determine the cause and possible cures of diseases that seem to infect these ladies of the night, as we refer to them. They unwittingly infect and are infected by their encounters. And of course, this infection is transmitted to the unborn fetus, which can result in either the death, or possibly worse, the birth of a defective child. We examine tissue and blood samples, trying to isolate the cause … but it is time consuming, and very costly. Many of the laboratory assistants are medical students not quite fully trained for this type of research."

"Does the French government offer any financial funds or grants for such worthy work?"

"Yes, but there are many research facilities and all are as desperate for funds … as we are, Dr."

While we continued the tour, I asked many technical questions so as to distract Dr. Ormon while I made visual observations of my own.

Meanwhile Holmes and Madame Fontaine had doubled back to Dr. Ormon's office where they were reading his file papers and case notes, when they were interrupted by two attendants of gargantuan proportions, well suited to restrain unruly patients.

After the better part of an hour, Dr. Ormon and I returned to his office where we sat and I talked about the clinic's medical facilities, which I found to be quite modern and in some cases, far advanced of many of the medical establishments that I have seen and in which I conducted my practice.

Dr. Ormon was quite pleased with my response and leaned forward over his desk to get down to the business of our contribution. "I have never heard of your organization. What did you say its name was, Dr.?"

"I apologize for that omission, Dr. The charitable organization we represent prefers to be very discreet and selective due to the many charities in need of money. However, I will be happy to tell you and would appreciate your discretion. The name of the organization is 'The Whitechapel Foundation' for the care of destitute women."

At the mention of Whitechapel his face twitched ever so slightly. I had struck a sensitive nerve. There was now a moment of silence as Dr. Ormon slowly sank back into his leather cushioned desk chair.

I took advantage of the moment to examine the many framed medical certificates and awards mounted on the wall behind his desk. "Your many awards are impressive, Dr. I can appreciate the scope of your work even more." I started to rise from the chair to examine the wall more closely when the doctor interrupted.

"Merely meant to impress our patients, Dr. Blair. I do not attach too much importance to them as I am sure a doctor of your medical background and service in the military must have equally impressive credentials. Did you not say you served in Afghanistan?"

"Yes, in the medical corps, and you, Dr.. I see by this certificate of appreciation that you served in the Crimean War of 1853 to 1856. Also I note you specialize in the field of human biology."

"The war was an experience that offered tremendous medical opportunities to advance the cause of human biology. Unfortunately, war is a mixed blessing."

"Yes ... Dr. I couldn't agree with you more." I tried to appear calm. I was beginning to be concerned about the absence of Holmes and Madame Fontaine.

"Now about your contributions to our clinic. What amount would your organization care to contribute?"

"Nothing, for the moment, Dr. We will report our findings to our Board of Directors for their decision, and I can assure you, Dr., it will be a favorable report. Now, if you don't

mind, we must take our leave ... as soon as Mr. Sacker and
Madame Fontaine return."

"I am afraid that will not be possible at this time as your
comrades are being restrained for the moment." He walked
over to a side door of his office, opening it wider to reveal
Holmes and Madame Fontaine bound and seated in two
chairs alongside which stood two large white-suited male
orderlies.

Realizing the failure of our play-acting, I started to reach
for my revolver in my back pocket. One orderly easily
restrained my movements grabbing my wrist and twisting
my arm back beyond its physical design limitations.
Holmes eyes widened and his head motioned to his cane
standing in the corner.

I understood his intent and wrestled my hand free, dropping
the revolver to the floor. The orderly turned, slowly moving
toward me. I ducked under his closing viselike grip,
snatching the cane in both hands and quickly unsheathed
the long blade, holding it at eye level directly at the orderly
who stopped short of impaling himself. I backed up, picked
up my revolver and proceeded to cut Holmes and Madame
Fontaine loose from their chairs.

Holmes took the sword, moving the orderlies back against
the study wall. "Excellent work, Watson!" He moved
toward Dr. Ormon, moving him away from the desk, ...
"And now, Dr. Ormon, or is it Dr. Kosnov, the famous
Russian war criminal who is wanted for the murder of
countless British soldiers who were prisoners of the
Crimean War. Your horrible experiments with these
helpless soldiers are well known, Doctor. You are a hunted
man who took the identity of the real Dr. Ormon. some
years back and undoubtedly you have murdered him as
well."

"Holmes," I shouted. "This is incredulous. We must report this discovery to the authorities at once."

"You are quite correct, Watson, but first we must safely remove ourselves from these premises."

The three of us started to back out of the study door and into the outer hall when suddenly a deep growling voice was heard to say, "Stay where you are, Mr. Holmes. I have a sizable blade at the delicate throat of your lady friend."

We turned to see a large man of obvious military bearing sporting a generous mustache which curled upwards at the ends. Holmes turned his blade on the man as he spoke, "Col. Moran, I presume?!"

"Yes, and you are Sherlock Holmes, the famous consulting detective ... and his friend, Dr. Watson. How convenient to have you both here. Now put down the blade, and give me the gun, Dr. Watson, or I'll put a bloody smile on the lady's throat."

We stood motionless as Holmes was undoubtedly reviewing all possible escape options. "You won't kill your only hostage, Col. Moran; we are all at equal advantage."

"Then, we will take our leave and the lady comes with us as a hostage, and you will maintain your silence if you want her to live."

We all walked cautiously to the waiting carriage whereupon Col. Moran threw the driver to the ground as the two orderlies took his place. "Don't follow us or we'll throw a pretty body out of our carriage."

We stood there helpless as we watched the carriage disappear down the wooded road. "Holmes," I shouted.

"Quickly, we must give chase and save Madame Fontaine. Hurry or we will lose the trail."

"Do not worry, Watson. I know where they are going and we will follow at a safe distance. Tonight we leave for Switzerland and travel on to the Reichenbach Falls and castle. There we will find the spider whose web we have all been entangled in. Come, Watson, I will explain the whole ungodly plot of Prof. Moriarty as we travel."

The steep incline stopped above the great abyss into which plunged tons of ice and water from the mountain river above. I felt my earlier resolve to rescue Madame Fontaine weaken. Was my courage beginning to freeze as well, in this icy hell?

CHAPTER 7

THE REICHENBACH CASTLE

That evening on the train to Zurich, Holmes made good his promise to reveal the whole Ripper mystery.

"It is a ghastly tale, Watson."

The Russian doctor is a biologist who was noted for his discoveries in the area of genetics ... the science of cellular heredity. He has successfully experimented with prisoners of war and is now experimenting on the prostitutes, who, in a drugged state, knew nothing of the medical procedures performed upon them. He is attempting to utilize cells from Moriarty's blood and tissue that will produce an exact duplicate... or more precisely, an original of the original...

The eggs of the prostitutes were only inseminated with Moriarty's cells after all of the women's genetic coding had been chemically destroyed within the egg. From that point on they were merely the vessels to carry the seed. The prostitutes were never meant to carry the fetus to full term; the women were only utilized to determine if the implantation of the cell would develop into a fetus.

Once it was determined they had succeeded, some several weeks later, the women were marked for death.

The murders served two purposes. By disemboweling the victims and taking some of the internal organs for examination, they concealed the pregnancy of the victims and at the same time diverted the resources of the police, government ... and the press... to exert their efforts in the opposite direction, from their other criminal enterprises.

Moriarty and Dr. Kosnov have formed an unholy alliance in pursuit of man's oldest dream ... Immortality. The doctor has made astounding scientific advancements in the field of human anatomy and biology.

These fantastic medical discoveries were accomplished by unscrupulous experimentation upon prisoners of war and on civilians both male and female.

Many perished under his scalpel; others died a most agonizing death due to infection, disease, and deformity. The prisoners were little more than laboratory mice used in horrendous numbers to expedite the doctor's work.

He accomplished in a few years what might have taken a century under normal scientific controls...the transplanting of vital organs from one patient to another, without infection or rejection...genetic manipulation to alter the development of an unborn fetus...for better or worse.

Thousands perished for every singular medical success.

I could hardly believe my ears. I knew many of these experiments were considered feasible, but not for many years. After all, this is the 19th Century, not the Dark Ages of Ignorance.

I had seen some successful transplants of tissue and a finger during the war. "Holmes, are you saying that Moriarty is so enraptured with himself that he would replicate others like him for sheer vanity?"

"No, Watson, not vanity, but survival. He is without a soul.

"He would grow the crop and then reap the harvest as needed to supply transplanted body parts to himself. He would murder the children of himself as they grow into manhood, and cannibalize their body parts for any need due to injury, ill health or advanced aging.

"He intends to outwit even death. Astonishing! Is it not!? The man is both mad and a genius at the same time. One can only guess the length to which he has gone to achieve this."

"We must prevent him from completing his experiment, Holmes! The police must know what has occurred here."

"No, Watson. We will only give them suitable information pertaining to the murders themselves.

"I have my reasons and will make them clear to you at Reichenbach, when the final piece of the puzzle is put in place."

"But how do you know they are going to Reichenbach?"

"I found papers from the clinic records indicating experiments were conducted there, and a postmark on one of the victims' letters.

"Watson, we are not following them ... we are being led!"

The journey was long and tiring as we traveled by train to Switzerland and then the town of Luxembourg, Basle, and Geneva until our final destination, the remote mountain village of Merigen and then onto the Hamlet Rosenlavi near the Falls of Reichenbach.

I was tired, but anxious to rescue the Lady Fontaine. We found rooms at the Inn of Engliscien Hof, which were rustic, warm and comfortable.

Holmes assured me that no harm would come to her as long as she was a useful hostage. I accepted his logic as sound, but I was still unsettled about his remark on the train that we were not the pursuers, but the pursued.

"Holmes, should we not contact the local constabulary for assistance and storm the castle tonight?"

"We have no proof of crimes. What type of assistance do you think we would receive from a small village of mountain people? Very little, I fear. And more the worse for them if they tried to help us. But, I do not wish to risk your life. Perhaps it would be better if you waited here at the Inn.

I must take the castle by stealth. As you can observe from our window, the castle is highly nestled in between cliffs of snow and pine trees. An army couldn't make a respectable assault without many casualties, especially in the dark. This is a moonless night. I must know how far he has gone in his mad experiments."

I peered out the window just barely making out the castle turrets in the darkening sky as I said to Holmes. "The thought of Madame Fontaine in that eerie place will not let me rest easy this night. I'll take the first watch and wake you in three hours. I will accompany you to the end of this chase."

"Very good, Watson, we will depart for the castle at first light. Keep your revolver in close reach. They must know we are nearby."

As Holmes slept, I peered out the window at the dark clouds crossing the night sky, blocking out stars in small patches. The silence was deafening. The mounds of snow allowed every creature to move about without a sound. The only sound came from the burning log in the small fireplace in the corner of our room.

After awhile I could just hear the faint sound of the wind and a glimpse of the castle by starlight. I was grateful for the sound of a wolf call, which awoke Holmes. For a moment I felt completely alone in the whole world.

Now, I could feel the pull of sleep begin to weigh heavy on my eyelids. Holmes took over the guard and I was secure in the knowledge that I could rest under his watch.

At first light we arose from a restless sleep fully dressed, having slept in our clothes, prepared for any intrusion by Moriarty's henchmen. We had arranged for two saddled horses to carry us up to the castle summit.

The cold morning air cleared our heads as we began the steep climb, trusting somewhat in the knowledge that our sturdy mounts would find a suitable trail through the mounds of snow, protruding black rocks and tall pine trees.

The horses' breathed out balls of smoky air before us as they moved cautiously along the narrow ledges where any slip would surely mean a fatal injury to both man and animal.

Holmes signaled for us to stop as we approached the high rear wall of the stone castle. The stones and rocks, being ageless, spoke no clue as to its architects or builders.

The locals say it was built by an occupying Roman garrison many centuries ago; perhaps a place of exile for Roman citizens or soldiers who had fallen from the grace of their Roman emperors, or an invincible fortress from which to wage war on the numerous mountain towns and hamlets.

Either way, it was a formidable and intimidating sight, like a giant beast reaching through the mist to the gray skies with claw-like turrets.

"There is no access to the castle from here, Holmes!" I said.

He paused, then continued following the great wall, looking for any possible entry to the castle. Roaring sounds of the Falls below became louder.

We approached a ledge we could reach from the saddles of our mounts. We tied the reins to a tree limb. The ledge appeared to offer an excellent possibility by which to enter the castle.

I reached for the stone outcropping, pulling myself out of the saddle, turning only momentarily to look down the steep incline which stopped abruptly above the great abyss into which plunged tons of ice and water from the mountain river above.

I felt my earlier resolve to rescue Madame Fontaine weaken; was my courage beginning to freeze in this icy hell as well?

Holmes touched my arm, reassuringly. "Yes, Watson, it is a frightful sight. Now be a good fellow and help me up to the ledge."

The welcome distraction was enough to snap me from my fear, ... and thankful for it, for I found new strength and bounded up upon the ledge, helping Holmes as well.

We stood on the wide ledge looking down at our horses who stayed in place in the event we should need to make a hasty retreat.

We turned to see a narrow slit in the walls; perhaps a ventilation opening. We entered, moving through the dark and into a torch-lighted hallway from which hung pointed spikes of ice. We followed the narrow hallway as it widened into a balcony above the open room below.

A large firepit filled with burning logs blazed in the center of the room giving a small but welcome warmth to the table and four chairs, one of which was occupied by Madame Fontaine.

On closer observation, we could see the lady was an involuntary occupant. Bound to her chair by small ropes of twine as thick rope or leather would have frozen, her head was free to move and she was not gagged. We thought to move down the stone stairwell to the room below and release the lady, but we knew it was a trap, much like a tiger hunt ... a goat tied down as bait for the strike from the bush; only the tiger was to be shot from a treetop blind by the hunter.

Suddenly Holmes shouted out loudly, jolting me from my thoughts. "Prof. Moriarty. We are here. What is your pleasure?"

"Go back, Mr. Holmes!" Madame Fontaine shouted. "Go back. It is a trap!"

Holmes was unmoved by her pleas. He moved toward the staircase. "You have gone to a great deal of trouble to entice me to come here, Professor. Why are we deprived of your presence?" He paused for a reply as his last words echoed throughout the castle halls. There was no response.

Again Holmes shouted out. "Come now, Professor. Let us conclude the game. Show yourself!"

These last words were barely out of his mouth when a shadowy figure came into the light of the fire. "As you wish, Mr. Holmes. And suppose you and Dr. Watson do as well. ... and then we can, as you say, conclude our business."

He was a stern figure of a man with black hair and beard, standing squarely on two feet next to Madame Fontaine. His presence equaled that of Holmes, bursting with intellectual energy and confidence.

"Holmes," I whispered, "we must be careful." I gripped my revolver even tighter as he replied.

"Wait here. I will entertain our adversary's wishes for the moment." He started down the stairs, his manner was confident and defiant as the two equals faced each other.

"Undoubtedly you know I have deduced the reasons you have, shall we say, invited us to this place."

"I have! And you no doubt know most of the answers, but not all. That is your weakness, Holmes, your insatiable curiosity, some measure of which I share as well.

"You are much like a playful child who can only amuse himself with complicated toys. I gave you many toys to play with; ... clues to engage your mind in the pursuit of the Ripper."

The professor circled around Madame Fontaine as he continued to speak. The glow from the flames only added to his dark and sinister presence. "You have interfered with many of my plans. I shall not continue to suffer your presence in this world much longer.

"This remote castle above the Reichenbach Falls has been my secret experimentation laboratory ... remote and safe from intrusion by the police and superstitious village people. And now you are here ... at my convenience."

Holmes moved a little closer as he spoke. "Why did you commit the 'Ripper' murders yourself, Professor? You could have easily hired a professional fiend like the doctor, or Col. Moran, or perhaps you liked it. You are the "Ripper"."

"Moriarty's face flushed with anger as he spoke. "I am Prof. Moriarty, a mathematician of note and there is no equal in my profession. I am not the Ripper; I invented him, much like an equation, to assist in solving a problem.

"I was committing the mutilations with the assistance of the doctor whose surgical skills were required to do the more delicate procedures. The work was done with complete scientific detachment.

"Those creatures were not human; they were the refuse of the human race. They were diseased and inferior. I, at least, made their pointless existence serve some purpose. They were not pure enough to carry my seed, and I would not let such creatures pollute my experiment.

"I have brought you here so that I may enjoy your humiliation of defeat. You thought to stop me, but you failed miserably."

Holmes seemed to be deliberately taunting Moriarty. His obsession with the man was evident.

"You were not scientifically detached ... you could not help yourself. Why, you're out of control! Look at what you have done! Are you perhaps just a little doubtful as to whether you're in charge of yourself, or is it the "Ripper" that I'm speaking to now?" Holmes moved toward Moriarity

"You are speaking to your executioner, Mr. Holmes. And you have spoken your last words." He spit the words out like a striking cobra.

"You will hear my voice from the grave. Letters have been written." Holmes was defiant and still moving closer to his equally defiant adversary.

"It is of no importance. Your efforts will come to naught. I have already succeeded in my experiments. It is concluded for the present; 12 married women of pure virtue in different countries carry my seed, mistaking it for their husband's, who brought them to clinics seeking family aide.

"Their identity will never be known and when the fruit is ripe, I shall pluck it from the vine. You will be shot and left dead here in the castle. The hillside above has been mined with a timed explosive that will bring the mountain down upon the castle, taking it and your bodies into the frozen Reichenbach caldron below. There will be no evidence left of our work

"Now if you will excuse me I shall permit you to die." He turned to the shadows beyond the light of the fire, as Col. Moran and Dr. Kosnov came into the room.

I kept my revolver pointed at them. "Get the woman, Holmes. I'll hold them from here.

"Stay put, Gentlemen, and I use the term reluctantly. I'll put a hole in the head of the first man who moves. I am an excellent shot I assure you, but if you doubt me, I have no objection to demonstrating my marksmanship, although shooting is too good for you."

Holmes started toward Madame Fontaine, but Col. Moran was quicker. With a knife put to her throat, he declared, "Hold! Or I slit her from ear to ear."

I was unable to maintain my composure. I came down the stairs holding the revolver straight out at Moran, and yelling, "If she dies, you die!"

Moran and the professor began to laugh.

"Stand back, Watson!" Holmes stopped my movement. "The lady is not a hostage. She is employed by the professor."

I could hardly believe my ears. "Holmes, what are you saying? Madame Fontaine is the one who helped us solve the case. How could she be in league with Moriarty?"

"No, Watson! Madame Fontaine is not in league with the professor. Madame Fontaine is dead! This is Marie Jeanette Kelly, the French placur who recruited the women of Whitechapel.

"She is in league with the fiend of Whitechapel for the money and safety from the Irish rebels who have sworn her death, that is why the body of Madame Fontaine was mutilated beyond recognition. They knew the police would believe it to be Miss Kelly."

The colonel untied the woman as I stood dumbfounded by it all. "How did you know she was not the real Madame Fontaine, and why did you not tell me of your suspicions?"

"I'm truly sorry, Watson, but I wasn't quite sure until the incident at the clinic when she took me to Dr. Kosnov's office. She knew precisely which records to pull from the files.

"Further, when I examined the mutilated body of what we thought was Miss Kelly, I noted that none of her fingers bore the mark of a brass ring.

"Scotland Yard believes the murder occurred at 4 AM because a witness heard a woman cry, 'Oh! Murder!'. Would not a woman scream for help? 'Oh! Murder!' seems more logical if it was said by one discovering a body. The victim was most likely killed much earlier; and one report had Miss Kelly seen with a man as late as 4 AM.

"I had to know the whole truth even if it meant danger to my life. But I had no reason to risk your life, Watson. Her French and English, although excellent, could not completely hide the Irish brogue; and this information was also sent to Scotland Yard. Miss Kelly?"

With that, she leaped at Holmes, who held her clawing hands at bay and then threw her to the floor. She began to scream at the professor. "You were supposed to kill them all. Now what will happen to me when the Irish Boys find out the truth? You bloody fool! They will kill me!"

She was desperate and began to cry and plead with the professor who now stood over her.

"Do not fear, Miss Kelly. They will never hurt you ... or find you." She seemed relieved momentarily, until the professor continued ... "You will be safely entombed here with Sherlock Holmes and Dr. Watson."

She knew the meaning of his words as the fear once again welled up in her eyes. She was about to scream when the colonel's knife passed cleanly across her lovely white throat. For a brief second or two she stood silent, then the slit throat opened, unleashing a gushing flow of blood. Her eyes bulged wide open and then rolled back into her head.

Col. Moran threw the limp body of the lifeless woman into my outstretched arms causing the revolver in my hand to fall from my grip as I tried to prevent her fall to the cold stone floor.

Col. Moran then leaped upon me, holding me in a viselike grip, as the Professor and Holmes engaged in a battle of life and death; each man griping the throat of the other. I was able to break loose from Moran and reach for my revolver on the floor. I wanted the pleasure of putting a bullet into that fiendish brain.

He took out his own weapon, firing as he ran up the stairs to flee the castle, no doubt, by the use of one of our own steeds.

I fired several shots that just barely missed him as he disappeared into the dark. I thought better of continuing the chase as Holmes was fighting a lone battle with the Professor, as Dr. Kosnov stood cowering in a corner by the castle entrance.

I tried several times to get a clear shot at Moriarty, but the quick movements of both men made it a dangerous shot that might well find its mark in Holmes.

I shouted for him to stand clear. He looked up for a quick glimpse as Moriarty ran past him taking the Doctor and his large bag through the front castle doors and into a waiting two-horse open carriage. I leaped down the stairs as Holmes followed the Professor in close pursuit.

The Doctor and the Professor were in the carriage by the time I got to the front door. Holmes was quite close as Moriarty took the whip to the horses who dug their hooves into the frozen ground, pulling the carriage with a jerk, and a running start down the narrow road, past the castle and the Falls.

I saw Holmes reach for the rear of the carriage. He ran behind it barely able to keep his footing. Quite suddenly, he flew forward as his clutching fingers grabbed the edge of the fleeing carriage.

Unable to assist Holmes, I looked back to see if I could find Col. Moran. I could just barely make out the man on horseback climbing up through the snow. "Why is he not going down the mountain?" I thought.

Then the realization struck. He was going to set off the explosives prematurely, hoping to catch us all in the avalanche of snow and stone ... even if it meant killing his employer, Professor Moriarty and Dr. Kosnov.

I had to get clear and somehow warn Holmes, I thought. But no sooner had I yelled his name, than I could see both him and the Professor struggling inside the carriage.

The carriage by now was running down the narrow path, dangerously careening out of control near the edge of the Falls. I could see the reins clearly on the ground between the horses running hooves.

Suddenly Holmes was shoved out of the carriage and onto the backs of the running horses snorting heavy streams of clouded breath. It was a fearful sight.

The Professor was whipping out at Holmes who was sinking lower between running hooves.

Suddenly the mountain above exploded. I could hear the rumbling sound of the avalanche and the cracking ice and snow breaking away from the mountain . It came crashing down upon the castle which was now covered in a white cloud of snow, trees, and stone. The noise grew louder as the castle was uprooted from its stone base.

I ran for cover, I could still see Holmes on the ground, holding onto the reins of the horses.

The Professor and the doctor looked up to see the mountain descending upon them like a hungry beast. Their fate was certain and irreversible as was Holmes who would surely share that horrible death in the falls below.

I yelled out his name once more as if to say from afar, "Farewell!" I could see him reaching for something behind him under the carriage.

The castle exploded from above. Boulders flew through the air like paper balls. The windstorm that preceded the slide also tore up trees by the roots. I shall never forget the howling sounds of the wind and the roar of the avalanchc.

The Professor and doctor screamed out at the oncoming white cloud of death.

The horses suddenly separated from the carriage and its weight ... their speed increased dramatically in a dash for safety just on the edge of the deadly avalanche. Thank God! They were dragging Holmes with them; he was holding tightly to their reins.

The carriage was blown into the air above the deep gorge, then quite suddenly, it was sucked into the yawning white steaming mouth of the abyss.

I could hear their screams fading into the roaring bowels of the Falls as the mountain of snow, trees, boulders, and ice fell in upon them. The rumbling sounds of the mountain continued for many minutes and the white cloud of death hovered over us much longer than that.

Afterwards, back at the Inn, sitting stiffly with a hot cup of rum around a fireplace, Holmes made a most unusual request of me. We talked of the ghastly details of Professor Moriarty's plan and of the unsuspecting families that carried Moriarty's seed.

"Watson, when I wrote the letters to Scotland Yard, I omitted the details of the Professor's plan to replicate himself. They needed only know he was behind the murders. He is replicating 12 children to insure that some will survive accidental death and disease."

"Holmes, this is monstrous." I said. "All 12 children will be Moriarty."

"No, Watson. All children will be born innocent. We cannot be their judge; only God and history can do that. No good could come of it. It would destroy the lives of those 12 families, and we are not murderers. Providence and fate permit no other course."

"Yes, of course, you're right. But I fear for the future."

"Our business is our time. We can only hope that the future will take care of itself. In the meantime, I must disappear from London for a time so as to determine the identity of the mothers. It will be better if the world believes I lie at the bottom of the falls with Moriarty.

"My investigations must go unhampered as Moran is still at large. I call upon you, Watson, to convince the world of my untimely demise until I return. And return I will, with the names of the mothers and their children for you to record for posterity and the judgment of history."

"I did as he asked. I wrote an accounting of his death. The story was called "The Final Problem". Scotland Yard believed Holmes to be dead and sealed the "Ripper" file for 100 years rather than reveal the details. He left and almost 3 years passed before his return.

He was true to his words and the names are written herein for the future to determine our failure or success. At least we prevented Moriarty from continuing his horrible experiments, and the murder of the children.

I did note, however, that during the period of Holmes' absence, the lady from the Scandal in Bohemia case, was also reported to be traveling about the continent. I would like to think that they enjoyed a brief respite together.

It is only speculation, for he would never confirm my thoughts as he is too honorable a man to compromise a lady's delicate reputation. I can only say that Holmes held her in the highest regard. At the mention of her name his eyes would be a bit brighter as if he had another challenging case to exercise his mental powers.

I have recently married, and would hope that Holmes might do the same, for it is an irony of the highest order to know

*that Moriarty's seed has been sown, while the future could
be deprived of the Holmes' lineage.*

*Col. Moran continues to elude the police, but I have no
doubt he shall be apprehended shortly, bringing to an end,
our most astounding case, and God willing, nothing further
will come of it.*

Dr. John H. Watson
LONDON
January 30, 1892

I closed the back cover of the diary, not fully believing
what I had just read.

"Did you see it, Dave? ... the names?"

"Yes... Professor Moriarty will never know how well his
experiment succeeded, or how great was its failure. I read
all 12 names, but only one leaped off the paper at my eyes.

Born April 20, 1889, in Austria, in the city of Braunau,
a boy, to a Mr. and Mrs. Schicklgruber.

"I recognized the name of the parents. I also knew when
and where their son had died: He chose to use his mother's
maiden name and died in

Berlin, in 1945,
His name was ...
Adolph Schicklgruber Hitler.

The diary is proof of Holmes existence and the true identity
of the "Ripper".

For the writer of the diary could not possibly know about Hitler, who didn't come to prominence or power until 1933 as Chancellor of Germany, over 40 years after the last entry into the diary and at least 3 years after Doyle's death."

"Dave! They've got her! They've got my Veronica! They want the diary back or they'll kill her!"

CHAPTER 8

THE PRESENT

My mind was reeling with the images from the diary. It was all too much to absorb in one sitting. I sat back, staring at Harry. We were both speechless. Finally, Harry spoke. "Dave, the commercial possibilities are endless, and it's also our obligation to tell the world what we have found out."

"Look, Harry, I've got to mull this thing over. You've had two days with it. Let's meet tomorrow for lunch in Malibu. You look like you haven't had much sleep anyway."

"You noticed the luggage under my eyes! O.K., I'll keep the diary until then: tomorrow, Noon, at the SandCastle. This is the mother of all exposes, Dave; the big one that every journalist dreams about."

I saw Harry to the door and watched his car drive away into the long shadows of the late afternoon sun. I don't know why, but I felt as if I hadn't slept for days; perhaps it was adrenal exhaustion. The diary certainly had my pulse rate up. I made some coffee and settled into my easy chair. I pressed the TV remote to listen to the news in an effort to distract myself from thinking about the diary, but it was useless. I couldn't hear the sound above my thoughts.

That night sleep overtook me with less than usual ease; I slept a restless sleep, waking several times during the night to look at the glowing numbers of the digital clock on my bedside table.

Disturbing visions of the Ripper, Holmes, and the mutilated women kept flashing in my mind, until thankfully ... the first light of dawn cleared the visions away.

I slept a couple more hours and after showering, I dressed, did some work, then headed out in my utility vehicle to Malibu to meet Harry, ... you know, the vehicle everybody is buying instead of the traditional luxury car.

The ocean air was refreshing and the usual California sunshine made yesterday seem like a bad dream. This was reality! I pulled into the parking lot which lies just at the bottom of a side road off of Pacific Coast Highway. The restaurant sits on a small stretch of private beach and has windows across the back wall of leather cushioned booths facing the ocean and allowing patrons an esthetic California view of the beach and the scantily clad female sun worshippers. A small pier juts out into the ocean permitting a few fishermen to test their luck. I entered the restaurant and took off my sunglasses, allowing my eyes to adjust to the dim light of the interior bar where I knew Harry would be waiting.

"Over here, Dave." I turned to see Harry sitting at a small corner table and hoisting a Bloody Mary. I sat down as the waitress returned with a greyhound for me. "I ordered for you, Dave."

"Thanks! I don't suppose either of us slept too soundly last night." probing Harry to see if the diary had a similar effect on him.

"I haven't had a decent night's sleep since I met the members of the Baker Street Society."

"Harry! You can't be sure their investigation of the authenticity of the diary has been proven. After all, you only have their word for it."

"I'm a step ahead of you. Knowing my friend, Bill's, background and having worked with him in the service, I would be willing to bet on the authenticity of the diary. However, I've already made arrangements with the police crime lab and the local Museum of Ancient Records; they need not know the nature of the material they are authenticating. Besides, it would be remiss at best and just plain stupid otherwise not to check it out. Harry sat back, obviously pleased with himself at anticipating my concerns. He was always pretty good at second-guessing me.

I leaned forward to give my words force. "Harry, even if the diary is authentic, who would believe it? We'd be a tabloid joke ... the Ripper, Hitler, immortality, and Sherlock Holmes. Sure it would get a lot of attention, but it's too preposterous. By the time the talk shows got through with us, we'd be lucky to work at all, let alone, in this business. It would wreck our careers. Think about it!"

"But, Dave, we've got proof!"

"Proof!? Are you kidding? This is the nineties; the age of special effects. The courts' can't get a murder conviction with a video tape of the act. They would just say our evidence is fake. It's a lot easier to erase history than to correct it. Remember the Neo Nazi groups that said the holocaust never happened? If someone wanted to say World War II never happened and all the news reel footage records and photographs were fake and living witnesses were liars, there would be some ... perhaps thousands ... that would believe it. Hell! We're a world of skeptics."

I leaned closer from across the table. "This country lost its naiveté after the JFK assassination and became a nation of pessimists after the Warren Report and the endless books about who killed the President ... Perhaps I should write a book about 'Who Didn't Kill JFK' ... the scenarios are endless.

"When I was a young reporter, I was a little pessimistic, I still believed in our government. Then came Watergate, the cherry on the sundae, and what I believe was the coup de grace to our government's credibility ... it's been downhill ever since. The CIA, the FBI, and other government agencies ... all have scandals to hide. ... Do you actually believe our voice would be heard or even taken seriously against all that? And, if all this isn't enough reason to forget we ever saw the diary, what about the people who don't want the world to know? You said yourself, it might even be dangerous."

I pulled back in my seat, taking a sip of my drink, and waited for Harry's reaction. I could see I got through to him dead center. He was convinced. Harry was usually quick with the comebacks, but not this time.

He just stared down at the wet glass rings on the table and, taking a deep breath, he said. "You're 100% right, Dave. I suppose I just hadn't thought it through enough. But, Damn, it would have made a hell of a story. Although there is one more aspect of the diary I haven't told you about ... "

He was waiting for my reaction, knowing that he, too, had hit a nerve. "O.K., Harry. Let's see your ace in the hole; not that it's going to change my mind."

"Dave, the Society took me into their confidence about one other aspect of the diary. ... their investigation into the lives of the other eleven clones born in 1889; 10 are dead, and one is still presumed to be living ..."

Later, out on the pier and after the shock of hearing about the one clone named Victor Monroe still being alive, I queried Harry for more details about this new aspect.

"I don't know how they did it, Dave; considering the devastation of post war Europe, ... and I was there to see it. Most of the cities and towns were completely destroyed, but over the past 50 years' major efforts were made to restore the lost records, ... and although far from complete or accurate, enough was learned about the clones.

"Some lived lives of simple obscurity like most people. Still others made respectable marks in the fields of business, science, and education. However, in one instance, a criminal-type of some notoriety developed, proving perhaps that we are creations of our environment and upbringing after all. I suppose if I were born into a tribe of South American headhunters, it wouldn't be deer antlers mounted on the wall over my fireplace. Still, the killer blood strain ran through the veins of all the children. "

"Don't we have to know about the last clone, and the effect he may have had upon our time?" He turned and looked out at the horizon where the sea meets the sky. 'O. K., so maybe Harry was bating me,' I thought. He's trying to tantalize my sense of curiosity to a point of no return and he was succeeding. I was thinking the same thoughts as Harry, until the muffled ringing sound of his cellular phone interrupted our concentration.

Harry was slightly startled and fumbled with the phone as he apologized for the interruption. "Sorry, Dave. Damn phone. I told my office not to forward my calls ... unless they were urgent."

"Then perhaps it is urgent." I replied.

He flipped open his compact phone, irritated by the interruption. "Hello, this is Harry. Listen, Hilda, I told you not to ... who? ... what? ... Who is this? ... Veronica?? ... Veronica? ... Mr. Raven? ... Who the hell ...? Put Veronica back on the phone. Hello, Hello! ..."

His face turned ashen white. I took hold of his shoulders to steady him against the pier railing. He was listening to someone on the phone and then slowly flipped the phone shut.

His knees seemed to buckle, so I walked him over to a nearby bench. I loosened his collar and thought he might be having a heart attack from whatever the conversation was on his cell phone.

He sat there in a shocked state, mumbling, and just staring straight ahead, then quite suddenly he turned to me, gripping my wrist tightly and with a strength I didn't know he had, he jumped up and grabbed me. "Dave! They've got her! They've got my Veronica! They want the diary back or they'll kill her!"

"Who was that on the phone?"

"I don't know, Dave, I could hear Veronica's voice. She said, 'Dad, give them the diary.'" and then another voice got on the phone, a Mr. Raven ... he said ... telling me two members of the Baker Street Society died in a tragic auto accident, and that the same thing could happen to Veronica."

My own knees started to go weak as I sat down next to Harry. "I guess that answers the question of the diary's authenticity."

"He said for the two of us to wait for another call at my office in 30 minutes. The cellular phone is too public. He knows about you, too, Dave."

"That's not important now. Don't worry, Harry, we'll get Veronica back. But first, we have to make copies of that diary. It won't help to prove our story, but at least we will have the story and maybe there is something more important than telling the world about this story."

"What?"

"Stopping whoever is still conducting this mad experiment."

"You killed two people ... No! Exterminated them! ... and call it 'Pest Control'?"

CHAPTER 9

THE HOSTAGE

I followed Harry's Lincoln Town Car back to his office in Santa Monica. The drive along the Coast Highway would take about 15 minutes; time enough for me to think about the events of the past 24 hours, and ... as I did, I reached several conclusions, ... some highly speculative others I was certain of. Our cars drove into the underground garage of the Oceanfront office building. I had been here many times since I first met Harry.

I had written a magazine article on government overspending in the defense industry. Harry read it and immediately contacted me about writing a book on the subject. Harry had a good instinct for what the public would buy and he thought I had the talent to do it That was fifteen years and several books ago.

We had become more than just business associates; we became close friends. He was like an uncle to me. I knew his wife and daughter, Veronica, since she was a child. Her being in grave danger unnerved me as well.

We took the elevator to his Penthouse suite of offices, staffed by several clerks and a secretary. We walked, heading directly for Harry's private office. He spoke to his secretary without looking back. "Hilda! Hold all calls except from a Mr. Raven."

Hilda, a matronly type whose efficiency more than made up for her dowdy appearance, reacted with routine professionalism. Harry was always courteous and considerate to his office staff as long as they did their job.

He was a sucker for a good Pacific sunset and you couldn't find a better view than from Harry's private office, furnished modestly in good taste, traditional and casual at the same time. Two green leather couches and a glass coffee table were the centerpiece where we spent many hours brainstorming about new marketing strategies.

He was a first class publisher and his advice, although contrary to mine on many occasions, was usually on the mark. I always gave him two votes to my one in the marketing department, and he did the same for me with the writing.

The small bar in the corner of the room offered a variety of refreshments, but at the moment, neither of us was interested. We sat in the couches looking at the silent phone sitting in the middle of the table, waiting for it to ring. I touched Harry's shoulder reassuringly. "Don't worry, Harry, we will get Veronica back safely."

He patted my hand with his own; I could see he was very distraught. "If the bastards killed Bill and one of the Society's other members, why not kill us, too? How can we trust them?"

"Perhaps they wanted to make a point."

"They did!" said Harry, who stood up and started pacing the length of his office floor.

The phone rang and our hearts skipped a beat. Harry reached over and pressed the speaker button. "... Harry Chrysler ... ... speaking. Is this Mr. Raven?"

"Yes."

"What have you done with my daughter?? You can have what you want, but don't hurt her ... please!!"

"I will talk about your daughter's safety after I have given you instructions for the return of the diary. I presume Mr. Conway is there with you and is listening."

"Yes, I'm here, Mr. Raven, if that's your real name, and I would be most interested in your terms."

"Not terms, Mr. Conway. Instructions! Don't think for a second that you have any choices in this matter. No, Raven is not my real name. I must admit to a flare for the dramatic. Ravens are black and I thought 'Black', being the color of mourning was quite appropriate under the present circumstances. Your daughter's life is in great danger, Mr. Chrysler."

Mr. Raven's voice was forceful. He spoke with confidence and authority. Perhaps a military type? ... or a high powered corporate type? ... used to having his way? No! ... used to being obeyed. A no-nonsense ruthless type. This would be the first clue to building his identity profile. I started to write notes as Mr. Raven continued to speak.

"I will make my position plain. We do not fear your revealing the details of the diary to the world. After all, who would believe you. I'm sure this possibility has already crossed both your minds.

"However, the actual diary could become a lightning rod attracting much attention ... like the Shroud of Turin. It

would be more of an inconvenience than a threat.
Followers, much like the UFO loyalists, never cease in their
efforts to find the Holy Grail, so to speak. We think of this
situation more as 'Pest Control'."

"You killed two people ... No! Exterminated them! ...
and call it 'Pest Control'?" Harry yelled out.

"You will bring the diary in its total completeness to me in
New York City. Take the American Airlines 'red eye' out
of Los Angeles tonight. A limousine will meet you out
front at the baggage area when you arrive. Look for a
chauffeur holding a copy of the London Times newspaper.

"And, you may, if you wish, have Mr. Conway accompany
you on the journey. If even one page or part of the written
page is missing, your daughter's life is forfeited. I will
not tolerate any deviation from the instructions. Do not
inform the police or anyone else."

"What about copies? Aren't you concerned we might make
copies public?" I wanted his reaction.

"You would be branded as a fraudulent fool. Copies are
not proof, Mr. Conway. We wish our work to continue in
secret without the annoyance of curious interlopers."

"How do I know you'll keep your word about my daughter's
safety?"

"You will be able to see her in New York during the
exchange. She is, at the moment, untouched, but sedated
to keep her safely under control.." The phone line suddenly
went dead. We had been dismissed.

Harry punched the intercom button on the phone. "Hilda,
book a reservation on the 'red eye' to New York tonight ...
American Airlines. Hold it!" He looked over at me holding

up two fingers, so I gave him a thumbs up. "Make that two reservations. Dave Conway is going with me. "

"First class, Mr. Chrysler?" Hilda barked back.

"Of course, but take anything you can get. If it's booked, call the VIP Club at the airport. They'll be sure we get on, even if they have to boot a stewardess or two off. And if that doesn't work, get me a private jet!!"

"Yes, Sir! I will attend to it at once. Is there anything else? Are you all right?" Hilda knew something was wrong.

"No! Everything's fine. Just do it!" He got up and walked over to the window, looking out into the late afternoon sun shining on the calm Pacific. "I saw you taking notes, Dave. What do you think?"

"Well, I haven't put it all together, yet, but I got a few ideas. ... Why don't we talk about it on the plane? I should go home and pack a bag."

"O.K., I'll send a car for you. ...... what about the police?? Do you think they could help us? After all, two people have been murdered."

"I doubt it. What proof do we have? We only have a voice on the phone. We would have to tell them the whole story and they would lock us up. But it's your call. I'll go along with whatever you decide."

"You're right, Dave, let's wait!"

That night on the plane we had a couple of drinks to settle us down. Fortunately, we were able to secure first class accommodations and the flight was not crowded, especially in first class.

The lights were dimmed to allow passengers to sleep. The 'red eye' is noted for being quiet and very dull. The lack of activity is a far difference from the regular flight schedules that offer more food, and aisles full of moving cocktail bars, passengers working on laptop computers and making cellular phone calls from their seats... The contrast can be both enjoyable or unsettling depending on whether you can or can not sleep at 35,000 feet while traveling at 500 to 600 miles per hour.

This night it was the former. We needed the quiet, without distractions, to analyze the situation and make our plans.

"What about your notes, Dave? You said you might have something."

"Well, nothing definite, but there are a few interesting possibilities. Mr. Raven is very confident and authoritative. I don't think he's a messenger boy. He is probably one of the principals."

"What makes you think he isn't acting on his own?"

"I noted that several times during his conversation he used the words I and we. This would indicate both authority and co-conspirators. 'I will not tolerate any deviations from the instructions.' and 'We are not concerned about you revealing the contents of the diary.'"

"Yes, Dave. I agree! He is not acting alone. What else?"

"He's very formal in his use of the language; well educated; not a foreigner. He used the word limousine instead of the popular term 'limo', ... then he reverts to the words 'red eye', not really slang, because it's a generic term for late night flights. However, most New Yorkers would not use those words. 'Red eye' flights are associated with West Coast to East Coast flights. Could it be Mr. Raven lives and works on the West Coast?"

"He said Veronica's life would be forfeited if we didn't obey his instructions. Who would use the term forfeited instead of killed? Terms like forfeited and eliminated are more closely associated with terrorists, the military, or secret government agencies. ... and the London Times.

"Perhaps he had flown in from London within the past 36 hours. There would be a lot of passenger lists from a lot of different airlines; but, he told us to take American. I would start with the American Airline passenger list.

"I would guess he was educated at a military school like West Point or a university like Harvard, his age between 45 to 55 years of age, a worldly type, well traveled.

"He speaks of their work. What kind of work? It has to be in the field of biological medicine; that much we know from the diary. And we can narrow that field of medicine down to the study of biological aging ... and clones."

"I'm impressed, Dave. You are beginning to sound like Sherlock Holmes."

"An Investigative Writer's work is not much different than detective work. Details are important. I believe I can find these people. All I need is a little time. But first, we get Veronica back."

"Dave, I have arranged for a hand gun to be slipped to me in the terminal. I couldn't get one past airport security in Los Angeles, and I would feel a lot better having some protection in case things go wrong."

"I think it's a good idea, but be careful. We will probably be watched as we leave the plane, or we may already be under observation, by someone on this plane."

Harry's eyes looked over my shoulder scrutinizing the sleeping passengers. "If you're right, we better take turns sleeping and keeping a tight hold of this diary I've got packed in my jacket." He held his hand tightly against his breast still looking the other passengers over, and the stewardess as well.

"Who can sleep? I'll be awake all night, Harry. But let's keep an eye on each other throughout the flight. We are under the scrutiny of their eyes and ears."

I wanted to run, but I knew we couldn't make it to the limo. I started to have second thoughts about not taking Harry up on his offer to give me the gun.

CHAPTER 10

THE EXCHANGE

The deep red line of sunrise at 35,000 feet is beautiful and evokes an inner emotion of awe at the earth's marvelous construction and mathematical precision. The red line widens, becoming a bright orange color, and within minutes a white silver band blinding to the eyes reaches up to our level of flight.

Sleeping passengers wake to the aroma of hot coffee. Now the activity of normal flight time begins. Briefcases open and close, and the lap tops bring up data.

The Captain's voice is heard above the humming jet engines announcing our expected arrival time in New York Kennedy Airport at approximately 6:15 AM.

We both looked a bit worn and bearded, but our appearance was the least of our concerns.

The plane came to a stop at its assigned gate. We were traveling light, with only a carry-on so we were able to make a quick exit from the first class sections, walking down the ramp to the gate entrance and into the terminal.

We came into the passenger area crowded with morning travelers.

I recognized the young man walking in our direction. He was from Harry's New York affiliate office; one of the 'on-the-way-up Brooks Brothers' types.

He passed us by, correctly not showing any sense of recognition to Harry, whom he bumped slightly. The almost undetectable smile on Harry's face told me the weapon was in his possession, and I felt a little better as we hurried toward the street outside the Baggage Claim area.

The early morning traffic was just starting to build up as we both looked for the limo driver holding a copy of the London Times.

There were several limos pulling into the baggage area's inside curb. I could see a chauffeur at the far end of the claim area standing beside a medium-sized Lincoln limo and holding a newspaper in his hand.

We approached him, being cautious and worried that things might begin to happen fast. Everyone from the baggage handlers to the taxi drivers and travelers looked suspicious to us. We were overly paranoid perhaps, but we couldn't chance a misstep at this critical moment ... Veronica's life was on the line.

I could see Harry gripping the gun tightly inside his pocket. He was very capable of using it if necessary. He had told me many stories of his accounts during the war in Europe, and he was no stranger to firearms. As for myself, I had some experience with hand guns, purely for self-protection and burglars.

The chauffeur looked us over as we approached. He moved toward us and was about to speak when Harry anxiously walked past him to look inside the limo. "She's not here, Dave." Harry stood up looking in every direction for Veronica.

He suddenly grabbed the chauffeur up against the limo. "Where is she? Where is my daughter? You son-of-a-bitch! And Mr. Raven ..."

"Ease up, Harry, I said, pulling him off the chauffeur. "Let's hear what he's got to say."

The chauffeur was shaken, but I assisted him in collecting his wits by brushing his tousled uniform jacket back into presentable shape. "Sorry about that, Pal, but my friend here is a little nervous. Did Mr. Raven send you?"

"Yes, Sir. Are you Mr. Chrysler and Mr. Conway??"

"Yes. Do you have any message for us from Mr. Raven?" Harry asked having calmed down.

"My instructions are to give you this newspaper and drive you into Manhattan. I don't know any Mr. Raven. I'm just your driver." He handed Harry the newspaper.

"What's your name, driver?" Harry asked.

"Leonard ..."

"Well, then, Leonard, start driving." Harry said, and dove into the limo. I followed as the chauffeur shut the door. We drove out of the airport complex and onto the Long Island Expressway, heading for the 'Big Apple'. I raised the privacy glass between us and the driver.

"Dave, look at this newspaper. They circled a small news item at the bottom of the front page. The small headline read, "2 Men Killed In Flaming Auto Accident." Harry began to read out loud.

'A car driven by Bill Cromwell, and a passenger identified as ... Charles Potter, crashed in flames as it left the roadway at Kings Crossing just outside of London. The driver was speeding and apparently lost control of the vehicle. Both men were pronounced dead at the scene. Mr. Cromwell was a former intelligence officer in Her Majesty's service during World War II, and Mr. Potter was a bank executive at Liverpool Trust.' Harry was livid. He took out his .38 handgun.

"The bastards made them talk and then faked the accident. Poor Bill. He just wanted to set the record straight, ... and they killed him!" He started to crumple the paper, but I stopped him.

"Wait, Harry! What's the date on the paper?"

He uncrumpled the paper, showing it to me as we both examined it. It was the early morning edition and dated today.

"Harry, that could mean they left London in the morning, their time, but last night our time in LA They must have flown into New York about the same time we did. They said they had drugged Veronica to keep her under control.

"Taking a commercial flight would be too risky ... and that means they would have to go through customs. They would have to use forged papers for Veronica, so we'll have to look for a doctor with a patient.

"They could easily put her in a wheelchair, and they would have to have drugs in their possession to keep her under. Customs would not allow anyone but a licensed physician to carry drugs into this country except in a physician's bag."

"We will have a hell of a time getting that information from Customs, Dave. I could try to contact a couple of politicians I know."

"Forget it, Harry. I have a very good contact in Washington, DC."

"Yeah? Who?"

"My ex-wife, Lorraine."

"That's a bit of good luck!"

"One more thing puzzles me, Dave. How did Raven find out about the diary's existence? After all, it was just recently discovered."

"I've been thinking along the same lines and the only possible explanation is that the Society's search for the background records of the clones must have triggered a computer alarm response.

"Perhaps it was the Victor Monroe file. When one travels the international computer network seeking information, one is liable to meet unwelcome strangers."

Just then the limo phone rang. The driver answered the phone and after a moment tapped on the glass.

We pressed the window switch to lower it as the driver said, "It's a Mr. Raven for you, Gentlemen. You can put it on speaker phone in back of your arm rest."

We found the speaker switch, and Harry answered, "We're here in New York. Where is my daughter, Raven?"

"Patience, Gentlemen. We must first attend to the other matter at hand...the Diary. We must examine it to see if it is completely in tact, and then you will have your daughter back."

"Where is she, Raven?" I asked, "Can we speak to her? How do we know she is alive and safe."

"Your request is granted. Look out the window to your left."

We did, and alongside the limo, was a black 4-door sedan with darkened windows. We strained our eyes to see the occupants inside, then quite slowly the rear passenger window lowered just enough to let us see Veronica's sleepy face.

We quickly lowered our window and Harry yelled out to Veronica. "I'm here, Baby. Don't be afraid. We're going to give them what they want."

The window closed up on Veronica's face, leaving us all the more frustrated, but thankful she was alive and apparently unharmed. ... for the moment ... ... anyway. The sedan sped up in front of us, as Raven's voice came back on the speaker.

"Satisfied, Gentlemen? And now for your instructions. Your car will follow ours until we stop at a place of our choosing. Do not get out of your car or we will drive away, taking your daughter with us.

"You will not follow us or we will kill her before your eyes. You will give the Diary to your chauffeur to give to us, and then your daughter will be released, but only after we have examined the Diary."

"That's not acceptable!" I blurted out, holding Harry's arm tightly. "What's to keep you from taking both the woman and the Diary? And don't give me that bullshit about your word or honor."

"You are in no position to bargain, Mr. Conway. We have the woman. Are you willing to risk her life so easily?"

"No! But you didn't bring us this far ... to break off the exchange ... We must have some assurance of her safety."

Harry gripped my arm and his revolver even more tightly. There was an excruciatingly long silence before Raven answered.

"Very well. I will make a small concession. We will drive to Central Park. The woman will be seated on a park bench. She will not run as she is too drugged to do so.

"You will bring the Diary to the bench, and then sit next to her.

"You will give the diary to our man who will be unarmed. Our weapons will be sighted on you both until we have thoroughly examined the Diary.

"When we drive away, you may slowly return with the woman to your limousine. That will take you a few minutes and by that time we will be gone and out of sight.

"Any attempt to follow us or contact the police will result in a reoccurrence of this unpleasant situation except this time you will have nothing to exchange for the life of the woman ... or yourselves." Harry nodded his head silently.

"That's acceptable, Mr. Raven. Let's do it." The phone went dead and we continued to follow the sedan as Harry poked the chauffeur on the shoulder.

"Keep up with that car in front of us. And for God's sake, don't lose it in this traffic!"

"Look, Mister, there's something going on here that's not right. I'm just a driver. I don't get paid to get mixed up in your drug business or whatever it is you're into."

"Just keep driving, Leonard, and there's a hundred dollar tip in it for you, or do I have to keep this gun at your head?" Harry waved the .38 for the chauffeur to see.

"O.K., Mister, for an extra $100. you're the boss ... and please don't shoot me."

"I won't shoot you unless you don't tell me everything you know. Who hired you to pick us up?"

"Never met anybody. The office said everything was arranged by phone. Cash was sent over by messenger, and that's all I know."

"O.K., keep driving." Harry said.

"I don't trust them, Dave. Maybe you better take the .38."

"No! You keep it. You're the back up. If anything goes wrong, just be ready to get out of the limo in a hurry. I'll take care of Veronica."

We followed the sedan through the thick morning traffic crossing the Queensboro Bridge into Manhattan and up 59th Street to Central Park. It was still early; about 7:30 AM when we entered the Central Park Roadway.

I grew up in midtown Manhattan and have always had a love-hate relationship with the crowded city. On one hand it is a wonderland of excitement full of something for everyone: world class restaurants, hotels ... stores, entertainment, art, and architecture that defy the limits of gravity ... boats and yachts moving in the rivers surrounding Manhattan ... the Money Capital of the World, and yet it has its dark side: crime, garbage, traffic jams where pedestrians walk alongside cars, faster than the traffic. Yet, transportation is incredibly available to all: subways, taxis, buses on every main street ...

Central Park is the centerpiece of the city; the crown jewel. It occupies miles of the most expensive real estate in the world. A miracle of unabridged generosity by the city's forefathers who designed and designated the 'Park' for the use of the young and old to be enjoyed by the rich and poor alike: lakes, ponds, fountains...the zoo... concerts.

The roadway ran throughout the park, curving, naturally following the landscape. Bridal and bike paths would parallel the roadway in places.

There were few people biking and horseback riding at this early weekday hour. And here and there a jogger could be seen running on the walking paths.

Privacy for the exchange might be difficult, and perhaps to our advantage. Witnesses could be a problem for Raven if he decided to do his worst.

We came to a rest parking area just off the roadway. There were a few benches; all empty at the moment ...a fountain and a restroom building. The sedan parked at the end of the rest area. Our car stopped and the phone rang. We answered it before the first ring stopped.

"Yes?" Harry said.

"Your car will remain back where you are. Only Mr. Conway will get out of the limousine. At the same moment my man will accompany the woman midway to a park bench. He is not armed, but my other man in the car is. He will keep you in his gunsights until I have thoroughly examined the Diary. When we drive away, that is your signal that we are satisfied."

We were parked back about 50 yards from Raven's car. I turned toward the door preparing to exit as the rear door of the sedan opened. We could clearly see Veronica and a man, wearing a T-shirt, helping her to her feet. They stood for a moment, waiting. The man raised his arms and turned around showing us that he had no weapon.

"Dave, I don't trust these bastards. If you get a safe chance to run for it back to the limo, take it. I'll cover you."

I gave Harry the thumbs up sign that I understood. I stood outside the car as Harry passed the Diary out to me, keeping the door open. I walked slowly toward the man leading Veronica to a bench midway in the rest area.

Everything looked normal. Birds chirped, squirrels ran up and down tree trunks, and butterflies fluttered around the wildflowers ... and inside my stomach. What if this was a trap and he had more men lurking nearby, posing as joggers or bikers? My paranoia was out of control, breeding like wire hangers in a dark closet. I started to sweat.

We both arrived at about the same moment as Veronica collapsed in a sitting position. She was barely awake, and definitely disoriented. She wouldn't be able to make a good run for it. I decided it best to sit it out with her, hoping Raven would keep his word.

I handed the diary to the man, a tall rugged type with dark glasses, difficult to identify. He snatched it from my hand and walked back to the sedan. A man's arm reached out through the rear of the sedan window, taking the Diary, while the mailman I had given the book to, just stood watching us with those dark glasses that gave him the look of a robot.

Another minute passed while I looked Veronica over for any obvious signs of injury. "Are you awake, Veronica? Can you hear me, kid? This is Dave ... Dave Conway. Are you injured?

"Dave," she moaned. "Dave, I'm ... sleepy. Can't ... stay awake. Father, give them what they want, please!" she moaned. She was delirious and unable to communicate. We were sitting ducks. Harry could never hope to stop them if they wanted to kill us. I wanted to run, but I knew we couldn't make it to the limo. I started to have second thoughts about not taking Harry up on his offer to give me the gun.

The next two minutes went by agonizingly slow. I kept looking at my watch, the sedan, the man robot's glare still fixed on us, then back at the limo.

I could see Harry was half in and half out ... ready for any sudden movement by Raven's men. My muscles tightened up, ready to sprint toward the limo with Veronica over my shoulder. She was limp as a piece of unglued wallpaper.

Then ... out of the side of my eye I caught the glint of something shiny being passed out the window of the sedan to our waiting zombie who suddenly put just the smallest wrinkle of a smile on his granite face. I knew immediately and all too well what it meant. He had what looked like a long barrel revolver; with silencer attached. He started forward, slowly at first, then quickened the pace.

I looked back at Harry who was out of the car and starting to point his weapon at our executioner who was almost upon us.

Just then a group of about ten joggers came around the restroom building and onto the pathway. This was our chance. I sprang up as the joggers started between us and the gunman. I lifted Veronica with ease. Amazing what a little adrenaline will do for you when you need it.

A shot rang out as Harry fired a round in front of the joggers and at the gunman who was firing at us as we ducked into the limo. The joggers, scared and screaming, scattered into the bushes, giving Harry a clear field of fire. The man ran back to the sedan, firing back at us continually until he was safely in the sedan, which was already speeding away from the rest area into roadway traffic.

Harry sat back in the limo holding Veronica in his arms. "Veronica! Veronica! It's Dad. Can you hear me?" She just gave him a thankful drunken-like smile. Her glazed eyes rolled back in her head and she passed out.

I grabbed our chauffeur by the collar. He was lying prone on the floor in the front seat. "It's O.K., Leonard, they're gone now. Get back in the driver's seat and get us the hell out of here before the police arrive. We don't want to have to answer a lot of questions. Get us to the nearest hospital."

"Right! You're the boss."

Harry yelled out, "Lenox Hill Hospital; it's not very far from here ... Exit at 72nd Street. Her doctor works out of that hospital and won't ask too many questions. He's a friend of the family. I'll call him."

We arrived at the hospital in a few minutes. Harry gave Leonard $100 and told him to get lost and not answer any questions. "Beat it, Leonard. And keep your mouth shut. Us drug lords are very big at finding squealers and getting even."

The limo sped away, screeching tires as it sharply turned the corner.

Later in the hospital waiting room Harry and I talked about the events of the day. Veronica's doctor had arrived and assured Harry that she was out of danger and would he on her feet in a day or two. Harry was right; he didn't ask questions.

We went to the hospital lunch room for a welcome cup of coffee. Neither of us had much sleep. It was close to noon and it was obvious we were getting a little punchy.

"Dave, I want to thank you for what you did today in the park. If you hadn't been there ..." his voice faded to silence.

"Forget it, Harry. If you hadn't arranged for the .38 and covered our escape, none of us would be here. Let's get back to the business at hand; finding out who Mr. Raven is and what connection he has to the Diary."

"Dave, you said your ex-wife, Lorraine, could help us get a passenger list from Customs. Suppose you get started on that while I see what I can do here in New York."

"Right. I'll take the shuttle to Washington, DC I'll call Lorraine and tell her I'll be at her office late this afternoon. We were a bad-married couple, but we're still good friends. I'm sure she'll help."

"Are you going to tell her everything?"

"No!. Just enough to get her to help. You've got a bigger explanation to give to Veronica."

"I'll stay here in New York for a day until I get Veronica back on her feet.

"I'll have to tell her something. She'll be expecting a full explanation. I think it best she visit one of her out-of-town friends for a few days until we can sort things out. I'll stonewall her on a full explanation until then.

"Need a lift to the airport?"

"No, I've got to go to a bank to get some travelers cheques. Credit cards leave a trail. If I can find Raven, he can find me too." I turned to leave, talking over my shoulder as I walked away.

"I'll call you on the cell phone tomorrow … and keep alert. They might come back! It's better if you stay close to Veronica. I'll grab a cab to the airport."

"It … involves a crime … so vast that no one would believe it. And I have no proof."

CHAPTER 11

THE GHOST OF THE DEAD

I was running for my life through the thick brush; the beast was almost upon me, snapping at my running heels. I leaped for the top of a high wall as a flash of light struck the shaft of the long-bladed knife which was being thrust into my back. I hung there on the wall, not moving. I could feel hot blood running down my spine. I fell to the ground alongside all the dead women of Whitechapel.

I looked up at the full moon in a black sky. The Ripper stood over me in his blood-soaked clothes. He smiled; red saliva dripped from his mouth as he kneeled down to finish his work. I started to scream ...

"Sir! Sir! We've landed. All the other passengers have exited the plane. I'm sorry to wake you, you looked like you needed the sleep. Are you all right? Can I get you anything?"

I blinked my eyes and rolled my head toward the sound of the voice. "No, no. I'm just a little groggy. It will pass. Thank you!" I looked up to see the blurry face of an angel instead of the devil. "Thank you, very much! What time is it?"

"3:00 PM." she smiled that plastic, 'Have a good day' smile, but it was a welcome sight to be back from the dead.

I hadn't slept for twenty-four hours ... Nightmares always seemed to overtake me when I was physically exhausted. Perhaps the mind being exhausted as well, lets the monsters up from the cellar of our ID, the unconscious, to run loose.

Later, after I had a chance to freshen up in the airport washroom, I took a cab to the US Treasury Department where Lorraine worked as senior accountant executive. The Treasury Department is responsible for collecting taxes, engraving and printing money, and collecting duties on imports ... through the Bureau of Customs.

I had called her from the airport before I left New York. She was surprised but looking forward to seeing me. It had been two years since we were divorced. We were always a continent apart ... her on the East Coast and me on the West Coast ... or traveling somewhere digging up facts for a new book. We both should have known better. You can't be together 3,000 miles apart for ten months out of the year.

The passion was there, but we couldn't agree on geography. She wanted to stay in Washington DC to do her job and I wanted to stay in LA to do mine. I respected her wishes as she did mine and love became a lusty friendship. We could agree on geography when it came to sex. Sometimes, her place. Sometimes, mine. Today it was her place. She promised me a hot bath and a little home cooking. What a woman! I thought, 'Someday, I'll have to marry her again.'

The view of the city as you drive across the Potomac from Virginia is inspiring. The monuments have always awakened a little patriotic spirit in me, putting a lump in my throat. Summer time in Washington, although humid, is beautiful. The Potomac River hosts a flotilla of boats to view the national shrines from a watery vantage point that doubles their reflected images in the calm water.

The cab pulled into the curb of the main building entrance. I paid the cabby and stood for a moment looking up the length of the building, trying to think how I would explain my visit to her satisfaction. She could be very difficult if my explanation wasn't convincing.

"Dave, Honey, you look terrible!" she said as I walked into Lorraine's private office. "Sit down before you fall down."

I took the easy chair as she came over and put her arms around my neck. We kissed a 'Hello' kiss and she sat on my lap. She spoke with a slight Southern drawl, having been born in Virginia. But she was well-educated and spoke in a general American dialect slightly disguising her accent except when she would lose her temper, and say to me, "Oh! Hush up!"

She was a good executive, but even those conservative, well-tailored suits she wore could not hide a great figure complemented by her wavy auburn hair and green blue eyes. "Listen, Lorraine, I need your help very badly. Oh, and you look great, Baby! Is that a new hairstyle?"

She got up off my lap and walked around to her desk to assume her roll in an official capacity. "Well, Honey, you know whatever I can do, I'll be glad to help, but I can't give you any official information ... it's against Department policy. When you called, you asked me about getting a list of transatlantic flights that landed at Kennedy in the last 24 hours, and went through Customs. I did just that!" she pointed to a file folder on her desk.

"Now, before I stick my neck out, what's so urgent that you need this information? If it's for another book, forget it. You'll have to make a formal request through channels and that's going to take weeks at best."

"Look, Lorraine. Just believe me when I tell you it's not for just another expose. It's life and death. That's all I can tell you."

"Dave, if it's that urgent we can bring in the police or the FBI and cut through the red tape. Especially if it involves a crime."

"It does involve a crime. A crime so vast that no one would believe it. And I have no proof. Just believe me when I tell you that I have to have that information now." I reached for the folder. Lorraine quickly slammed the palm of her hand down on top of it. I looked across the desk at her. Our eyes met and spoke to each other. She must have seen the urgency in mine.

"No, Dave! I'm sorry, I can't do it. You come struttin' into my office and expect that a few simpleton compliments will melt me down like ice cream in July." I brought my hand back off the folder. She stood up. "This is official information. I have no authority to let you read it. Now wait here, I'm going to the ladies room …"

I started to open my mouth, but she kept talking. "… and when I get back I'll expect you to forget about this information on my desk, and then we'll go to my place. Stop drillin', Honey. You've already struck oil." She smiled and left me alone in her private office with the file folder on her desk.

That evening, back at Lorraine's Georgetown house, I got that hot bath and home cooking she promised, and both were sorely needed. I shaved and rested for an hour before dinner, and felt much better, but I could still use a few hours of sleep.

We had a candlelit dinner of pasta, garlic bread, cheese, wine, and a dessert of strawberries and cream. It was all so normal. Yesterday seemed like a hundred years ago.

The townhouse was a two-level structure with a small yard and a single-car garage. She had bought it herself several years ago and furnished it in Early American with a few modern decorative touches ... green and blue; her favorite colors ... all earth-bound shades. I always felt comfortable here and often wished I could transport the townhouse and Lorraine to California.

I wore a bathrobe that Lorraine kept for me to use when I'm in town. I walked over to the window, still a little cautious and paranoid, to see if there were any suspicious strangers on the street.

Georgetown is colonial in appearance and only the well-heeled could afford to live here in their vine-covered brick townhouses. Everything looked right; people out for a summer evening stroll; cars; nothing out of place ... almost too perfect.

My heart started pumping wildly and I started to shake a little. Lorraine placed a hand on my shoulder and nibbled the back of my ear. It brought me back from the brink, and settled me down as I turned to kiss her. "It feels good to hold you in my arms again, Lorraine."

"Ditto." she said. Then she took me by the arm to the most comfortable couch in the world, to sit down. We had picked it out together. "Dave, you've got to tell me what's troubling you. Perhaps I can help."

"You can't ... and you've done enough already. I can only tell you that it's dangerous and I don't want to get you involved. Two people have already been murdered."

Shocked, Lorraine drew back from me, struck, no doubt, by the enormity of what I had said. "Dave, if your life is in danger, you must tell the police about the murders."

"I can't! No one would believe me; I can hardly believe it myself. I've already told you I have no proof. Trust me in this."

She leaned forward into my arms, and we held each other close, and tightly, as if afraid a strong wind would blow us apart.

"Lorraine, I want you to do one more thing for me and don't ask me why. Just do it! I may be sending you a manuscript detailing the events of the past three days. It is vital that you hide it in a safe place. Don't read it. The less you know, the better.

"But, if you should not hear from me within one week after you receive it, you may presume I am physically unable to contact you, or I am dead." Her eyes widened, and she started to speak, but I cut her off. "At that point in time you may read the manuscript and use your best judgment as to its use. Believe me when I tell you, I'm not doing you any favors by involving you in this strange odyssey, but I want some record of this story to survive even if I don't."

We didn't speak further of the manuscript. We went to bed and made love, holding each other as if it was for the last time. I sank my head into her beautiful full breasts. I wanted to lose myself inside her. I wanted to be one with her. My trembling body stiffened as I began to feel the sensation rising in my loins ... her body rose up to meet my own. She clung to me tightly, moaning in her own moment of ecstasy, and then I collapsed exhausted into her arms.

That night I slept peacefully in Lorraine's embrace. I felt safe and secure; the ghost didn't come back. I suppose Freud would have something to say about the 'mother complex', but all I know is that restful sleep with Lorraine recharged my body and my mind.

Things seemed clearer that morning. I looked at the clock; both hands were on the 12. It was daylight, so it must be noon. Lorraine had already left for the office. I told her last night I was leaving in the morning and would keep her advised. She left me a note.

'I love you ... take care ... God bless! And come back to me soon.' Lorraine, xxx ooo, kisses and hugs, mi casa su casa.'

I dressed, drank a cup of coffee that Lorraine had left for me in the microwave, and headed for the nearest library where I would look up some medical definitions on cloning. Then to the airport to fly back to the coast and chase down two leads I had copied from the Customs' report.

"The next time you hear my voice it will be in person and very likely the last thing you will ever hear."

CHAPTER 12

SAN DIEGO

The cross-country flight to San Diego gave me enough time to collect my thoughts and make a plan. I called Harry's cell phone from the plane, not knowing exactly where he was. He answered immediately. "Dave, is that you?"

"Yes, Harry. I'm in flight on my way to San Diego. Where are you?"

"Back at my office; flew in from New York late this afternoon."

"How's Veronica?"

"She's fine, but pissed as a killer bee. She wanted me to call the FBI and Interpol. I had a hell of a time calming her down, but she finally cooled off after I told her about Bill Cromwell's death.

"I got her to visit an aunt upstate New York. Her husband's not due back from Paris until next week and he doesn't know a thing about what happened. She will sit tight for a few days.

"What about you? Did you find out anything from Customs?"

"Quite a bit! There were four flights; two physicians. One with a sedated patient in a wheelchair; his passport listed his name as Dr. Warren Frazer, a Biochemist."

"Sounds like our man, Dave. Is he in San Diego?"

"No. Santa Barbara. I'm seeing a Dr. Abramson at the Baylor Institute in San Diego. You'll remember, I did a story last year on the black market for human organs. He was one of my sources of information on the subject.

"I have a few questions I would like to ask him about clones. He's a noted biologist and all those doctors seem to know what their counterparts are up to all over the world; they all read the same medical journals. Perhaps he can give me a lead on our Dr. Frazer, and what kind of work he's doing. Did Veronica say she could recognize her abductor?"

"No. She went to the airport to make her New York flight and was told that there was a telephone call outside in a limousine. When she entered the limo, they chloroformed her. She was in a daze until we rescued her in Central Park."

"Harry, look up this Dr. Frazer in the Who's Who. See if he's got a clinic somewhere. I'll call you tomorrow morning.

"I'll be staying at the Hilton Hotel tonight on Mission Bay under the name of Segal. My plane gets in about 9 PM, West Coast time.

"I'll call you after I meet with Dr. Abramson in the morning. Oh! Book a car rental for me at the airport, I don't want to use a credit card.

Landing at San Diego airport is some kind of an experience. You come in low ... right over the downtown high rises ... that's West Coast slang for sky scrapers. It's dicey and the pilots must have stories to tell. But, it's beautiful at night, and like landing a magic carpet on the smooth mirror of the bay water.

I picked up the rental car and went directly to my hotel and to bed. I was both mentally and physically exhausted.

The next morning I drove up the coast about 15 miles north to La Jolla; a beautiful cliffside Beverly Hills overlooking the Pacific, populated by affluent retirees, tourists, artists, yuppies, and students attending the nearby university.

I slept on and off all night long, but was feeling clear-headed, and happy to be back in California. I arrived at the Institute about 10 AM, the agreed upon time for our meeting.

The Baylor Institute, like many of the California 'think tanks', sits unobtrusively into its surroundings, barely visible in spite of its size. The kind you drive by and wonder what the hell they do in there behind the glass-paneled walls reflecting its own surroundings.

Dr. Abramson had scheduled a 15-minute meeting time for us as his itinerary for the day was full. We met on the terrace of the cafeteria overlooking the ocean below the cliffs.

He walked briskly toward me, holding out his hand. "I never seem to tire at the marvel of this beautiful view, Mr. Conway. I hope you don't mind meeting here on the terrace instead of my stuffy office?"

"Not at all, Doctor. I like the fresh ocean air, and you must invite me back sometime to see a sunset."

"Anytime. We have an inexhaustible supply of fresh air and sunsets, and they are free. Come sit down. We will have some coffee." We both chuckled as we seated ourselves at the patio table already set with coffee and cake.

Dr. Abramson was in his mid-fifties and although he hadn't won a Nobel prize yet, most of his colleagues felt it would be forthcoming at any time ... his work was on the outer edge of biological science seeking out the unknown; sort of a Biological StarTrekker.

"Dr. Abramson, you will recall last year I interviewed you about the black market in human body parts."

"Yes, and I read your article with interest. It was very well done and I was very pleased that you did not misquote me. Now, how can I be of assistance to you? You spoke of another article on the cloning of human beings."

"That's correct, Doctor. I'm doing research on the subject, but the theories are becoming old hat. There have been dozens of newspaper articles, books, and television shows on the subject and the collective opinion, including your own, is that it is not only feasible, but inevitable."

"Yes, Mr. Conway, that is the consensus of the scientific community. When, not if, is the question. The cloning of body parts, and perhaps an entire body, is theoretically possible."

"That's exactly my point, Doctor. That's the angle I'm interested in. The When! I'm looking for the scientists that are breaking new ground, ... scientists like yourself. Frontiersmen, so to speak."

"That shouldn't be too difficult. There are perhaps a dozen or so scientific groups worldwide that are credible organizations fitting your criteria."

"Doctor, we know there is a demand for vital human organs. What could an unscrupulous scientific organization accomplish in this single experimentation if they were unrestricted by moral or legal conscience. Say, ... like the Holocaust scientists and their experiments on human prisoners."

"That would be a scientific nightmare; experimentation gone wild. Loss of life, freaks of nature ... It's unthinkable!"

"But what of the results? Could advances be made in, say, a tenth of the time?"

"Unrestricted use of human guinea pigs would accelerate the results and after-effects by perhaps that much. Even having achieved a success in cloning a perfect human specimen, it would take years of study to evaluate data. Perhaps the full lifetime of the clone itself.

"In science when we open one door of enlightenment, we find several more on the other side of the threshold. It boggles the mind, and there is no one predictable result. Are you familiar with the 'Chaos Theory', Mr. Conway?"

"Somewhat." I said. "I believe it refers to the relevance of a butterfly flapping its wings in the Amazon and having a connection to a tornado landing in Kansas."

"That is correct. All things in the universe, singularly in motion. Unrelated events, yet collectively affecting the entire world and cosmos. The domino effect ... in constant motion. Never-ending. You leave your home in the morning and perhaps your entire life is changed completely, depending on whether you turn left instead of right at your street corner. Perhaps even history itself."

"Wow! Doctor, it's too much to conceive."

"That's why it's called the 'Chaos Theory'. Believe me, young man, it is better not to think about it too long or you will end up talking to yourself like the rest of us scientists." We both smiled and laughed a little at the thought.

"I see your point, Dr. It will make an interesting piece for my article." He looked at his pocket watch, indicating to me politely that our time was almost up.

"Well, I won't take up any more of your time, Dr. Abramson. Is it possible I could see that list of organizations you spoke of? I'm sorry to press you, but I would like to return to Los Angeles this evening."

"Of course. I'll have my secretary make up a list for you. It will take maybe a 1/2-hour. Why don't you stay and enjoy the view. I have a staff meeting to go to. " He stood up as we shook hands.

"Thank you, Dr. I'm very grateful for the time and your help. Oh! One other question. Are you familiar with the work of a Dr. Warren Frazer, a bio-chemist like yourself?"

He looked down, then up to the sky. "No-o-o, I don't believe I have any recollection of him. Ah! But at my age people start to think of me as the proverbial absent-minded professor."

"I'm sure that catastrophe will never overtake your brilliant mind, Doctor."

"You are too kind!" he replied. He started to leave, but stopped as if a new thought had popped into his head.

Then he turned back to me and said, "You know, I just happened to remember. One of the organizations on that list is very close by ... in Palm Springs, I believe. I'll tell my secretary to mark it for you." He turned and walked briskly away.

I sat for a while sipping what was left of my coffee, made cool by the ocean air. The time past quickly. I was anxious to see the list ... as I felt Dr. Warren Frazer's name and organization would be on it. And my search for Raven would be coming to an end.

A very attractive and statuesque woman, wearing a smartly tailored suit came out onto the terrace. She carried what I guessed to be the list of clinics. She had a severe but very efficient look about her. She was clinically beautiful.

She gave me a mini-smile as I stood up to meet her outstretched hand holding the folded single sheet of paper. "Mr. Conway, Dr. Abramson asked me to prepare this list for you."

"Thank you, Ms. ..."

"Fleming." she smiled. "I'm the doctor's personal secretary. Do you have any questions?" She noticed my grin and added, " ... about the list?"

I opened the sheet of paper on which were about ten listings of clinics and the names of the head administrators. Frazer's name was not there. "Is this the complete list, Ms. Fleming?"

"Complete only within the parameters of the criteria you requested. There are many more, but none in the area of cell replication and cloning."

I lowered my eye back to the list. "I see a health spa in Palm Springs marked. Is that an error, Ms. Fleming?"

Her eyes widened and her teeth gritted together in what must have equaled the jaw pressure of a great white shark's bite. "It is not an error! If you look more closely you will see a small note indicating a research department as well."

"Oh, yes! I see it. I'm terribly sorry." I put out my hand to shake hers as I said, "Thank you very much, Ms. Fleming. I won't take up any more of your valuable time."

Her grip was worse than her bite.

I was happy to be out of the place and on the road ... to Palm Springs. I called Harry from the rental car phone as I drove east to the desert.

"What the hell do you mean there's no listing of a Dr. Frazer? Harry, he came through Customs. God, dam'it!?"

"Dave, he could have had a fake passport. If he did, that puts us back on our own one-yard line."

"Not quite! We know he's a medical man and I'm sure I can get a lead on his lab if he has one here in America, and hopefully, in California, which I'm sure he does. ... Keep trying, Harry! ...

"I'll stop at the nearest postal and fax service center and send you a copy of the list of clinics I got from Dr. Abramson. You might come up with a lead. All the clinics are engaged in experiments of rejuvenation, and cloning of cells. He's got to be close to one of these organizations."

"When do you get back to LA? I've got a hunch Raven will be waiting for you. You'd better not go right home."

"Right! I'll call you tonight. I'm on my way to a health spa in Palm Springs."

"Really, Dave! Don't you think this is the wrong time to be pampering yourself like a Hollywood star?"

"Don't be ridiculous! The spa is on the list and it has a small research facility."

"Sorry! I'll be here at the office the rest of the day. Call me tonight."

"Oh! I just had a thought. Call Lorraine for me. She knows I need help. Find out if this Dr. Frazer had a flight to France or England from America a day or two earlier. If he lives in Europe there should be no record of a previous flight.

"If there is, then that computer alarm set off by the Society searching the records must have rang the alarm bell here in Southern California."

I sent the fax to Harry and called ahead to the Temple of Isis Health Spa on the ruse that I was referred by Dr. Abramson and in need of their impressive rejuvenating services.

The drive from San Diego is only a couple of hours and they were expecting to see me about 2 PM. I'd had a difficult time getting an immediate appointment, as there was a long waiting list. However, if Dr. Abramson referred me, they would extend to me a little professional courtesy on his behalf.

It was off season in Palm Springs. No one in their right mind goes to the southwestern desert in summer where the temperatures can reach 115 degrees Fahrenheit.

The people who live and work in the "Springs" during the summer months, don't go out until after sundown. A shaded parking space is something 'to kill for'. Most of the wealthy residents left town three or four months earlier for more humane temperatures. The town would be a little less crowded and only the suicidal would decide to play a round of golf on a hot day like this.

Even the air-conditioning of my rental car struggled to keep the internal temperature below 85°. I hadn't planned on staying overnight, but if I did, hotel rooms would be plentiful and at reduced rates.

I pulled into a restaurant parking lot to grab a sandwich and decided to call my answering machine for the messages that might be piling up. I kept the motor running to keep the car cool. I dialed a 4-digit code that would activate the machine to spill its guts.

"Hi, Dave! It's Madeline; in town for a couple of days ... thought we might get together for lunch. Call me at my club. Bye!" Tues. 10 AM.

And so it went on for the next five or six calls ... friends, my attorney, a sister, and my CPA. I began to realize how much of a common man I was ... cable TV, answering machines, car phones, faxes, a laptop computer, and a Power PC. But I wouldn't have it any other way ... and it was all tools of the trade ... and perhaps they could help me in my search. My meandering thoughts were suddenly cut off as I heard the voice of Mr. Raven.

"Are you looking for me, Mr. Conway? Are you getting closer? Be very careful, you just might find me ... unless I find you first. I know you are back in California; that was clever of you not to use credit cards. It does make it more difficult for me to find you, but not impossible.

"I apologize for that ugly business in the park; one of my men over-reacted. Perhaps you should forget this unpleasant business and get back to your normal life. At least to what's left of it. The next time you hear my voice it will be in person and very likely the last thing you will ever hear.

The answering machine gave the time of the call as 11 AM this morning. Was Raven playing a guessing game? ... trying to unnerve me? Naturally, he could assume I would return to California. He found out my unlisted phone number; he must also know where I live.

Harry was right. I can't take a chance on going home just yet. I'll have to buy some fresh clothing. I haven't been in one place long enough to get cleaned what few things I packed into my carry-on bag three days ago.

My mind was racing with thoughts. Who could I turn to for help? Who could I trust? What if he does find me? And what, exactly, could I do if I find him?

Slow down, I thought. Raven has got you bouncing off the furniture. I won't play into his game. Keep focused. Find Mr. Raven.

If his experiments are illegal, report it to the scientific community and the police. And, above all, try to stay alive!

"What's to become of a society where the rich cannibalize the 'have-nots' for spare parts?"

CHAPTER 13

THE TEMPLE OF ISIS

I followed the directions I was given and found the Temple of Isis Health Spa on the outer edge of the business district. It was set back in the foothills surrounded by date and palm trees, pools of water, and fountains decorated with statues of the ancient Egyptian gods ... Isis, as I remember, was the powerful Goddess of fertility and life.

I parked in a shaded area of the half-empty parking lot and walked up the stairs of the Temple-like structure. The Egyptian architecture did not seem out of place; it blended beautifully with its surroundings.

I walked on green tile floors through flowing curtains of pink gossamer, getting cooler with each passing step until finally I entered a large open circular room. At its center was an oval reception desk covered with jade figures, urns, and hieroglyphics. Not having a Rosetta stone and kidding myself to relax, I decided not to attempt an interpretation of the figures ...

Two lovely nymph-type females wearing thin transparent togas sat at their work stations; one taking calls and the other monitoring a computer with several closed circuit television screens. It seemed strangely out of place. I found it difficult not to look at the taunting loveliness of these beautiful women.

The top of the circular room had 360 degrees of tinted glass windows allowing light to pour in from every angle. Seven bronze doors, separated by hallways, stood beneath the windows.

"Good afternoon and welcome to the Temple of Isis." said the nymph who had just put the phone down.

"Good afternoon. I believe I am expected. My name is Dave Conway."

She looked down at the computer screen. She smiled and said, "Yes, of course, Mr. Conway. Would you please follow me to our private conference room?"

She came around the desk and walked me over to one of the doors. She pressed numbers into a small keyboard access control unit.

The door slid open revealing a conference table with six chairs, a television monitor, and another door at the far end. "Please be seated, someone will be with you momentarily."

The door slid shut. There was a pitcher of water on the table with a platter of fresh fruit beside it.

The TV monitor came to life and restful music filled the room as a voice narrated the wonders of the Temple of Isis. A sales pitch, I thought, to soften me up for the close, the cost of which I speculated to be the next 20 years of royalties.

After ten minutes the TV screen went blank, but mood music continued to fill the room.

The door at the rear of the room opened revealing a woman of youthful beauty covered in a transparent flowing toga. She was dark and had an ethnic look about her ... perhaps Italian or Spanish!

"Mr. Conway, I am Fiona, your guide to the new afterLife."

"Wait a minute, Miss ... Fiona. I'm here to get healthy, not embalmed and mummified." I laughed.

She smiled as she took my hand in hers and sat next to me. "Of course. I am speaking of your new life to come after you have been rejuvenated by our healing wonders of diet, exercise, medications, and if necessary, cosmetic surgery. I shall show you many miracles of rebirth that our completely satisfied clients have experienced."

She took a remote control from a compartment beneath the desk. She activated the TV monitor, and began to show me a variety of before and after photographs of both men and women.

The transformations were nothing less than spectacular ... old to young ... fat to thin ... sagging bags of skin to tight bodies. The mob and witness protection programs were probably among their best clients.

"These photographs are very impressive, Fiona, but after all, a photograph can be greatly enhanced. Could I possibly see any of these people in the 'new' flesh, so to speak?"

"I'm sorry, but client confidentiality is amongst our most guarded secrets. We couldn't very well ... But I'm sure you can appreciate our reasons." she said as she fluttered those extra long eyelashes shading her beautiful brown almond-shaped eyes.

"Yes, of course. I would expect that same consideration as a client. Could you tell me a little more about the special medications and the surgery?"

She reactivated the TV monitor, showing various photographs of treatment sessions. "The medications are the latest scientific discovery, beyond anything you can obtain anywhere. Hair and skin lotions, vitamins, hormone injection; all prescribed, all safe and medically administered by a registered nurse and physician."

"What does it cost for ... say for a two-week stay?"

"The cost varies depending on the client's needs, but an average would be $15,000 per week, and more if surgery and recovery are involved. Perhaps as much as $150,000 for a month stay."

I started to swallow a tennis ball size lump that was stuck in my throat ... so I could speak. It took a few seconds of mental arithmetic to do it.

"I would like to know more about the medications and the surgery. I wonder, might I speak to Dr. Trent, the head of the clinic?"

She leaned back in her chair, studying me. A sexy smile parted those luscious lips revealing pearl white teeth and pink gums. "You know, Mr. Conway, I don't think there is much to improve on in your case, ... but you could use a little work."

She looked me over, continuing to smile; her breasts pushed the delicate silk of her toga to bursting limitations with every inhale of air she took, and floated beautifully above her skin with every exhale.

"Thank you, but you're only looking at the outside. Inside I feel like a used car; leaky seals, clogged radiator ... I would still like to speak to Dr. Trent. After all, we're talking about a large sum of money."

She pressed an intercom button on the table speaker phone. "Is Dr. Trent available for a consultation. Mr. Conway would very much like to meet her."

There was a pause, then the receptionist's voice snapped back. "Dr. Trent is available to see Mr. Conway."

She shut off the phone, stood up, and extended her arm gesturing for me to walk through the rear door which was automatically opening into the interior of the temple.

I got up and walked to the door where a young Hercules waited, dressed in T-shirt and slacks. He was built like a coke machine with a head.

I turned back to Fiona. "By the way, Fiona, how old are you?"
She smiled broadly and pressed a button to close the door between us. "This way, Mr. Conway." said Hercules.

I followed my escort along a well-lit hallway of statues, urns, and flowers, until we came to a double set of tall floor to ceiling bronze doors engraved with more Egyptian hieroglyphics.

The escort pressed an intercom button to the speaker on the side of the door. "Mr. Conway is here, Dr. Trent."

The power doors opened inward. I entered the room alone and the great doors closed behind me. I began to feel like that Kansas girl, Dorothy, having entered the inner realm of the Wizard. It was a very large room, but no fire and thunder was apparent.

The handsome middle-aged woman seated at the desk rose to meet me. "Please be seated, Mr. Conway. I am Dr. Helen Trent."

She held out her hand and as I reached for it she appeared much younger in the light shining in from a skylight above the center of the room which was a departure from the Egyptian decor; ... more executive, traditional furniture, couch, chairs, serving bar, and a beautiful view of the mountains above us.

"Good afternoon, Dr. Trent. I'm quite impressed with your facility."

"We prefer to call it a spa. Facility is such an industrial word; like a factory."

"Yes, I see your point, but in a sense you are a factory turning out recycled people." She ignored the remark.

"Come, let's sit by the coffee table. It's more comfortable and I can answer the many questions you must be waiting to ask. I understand you live in the Los Angeles area.?"

"Yes, I'm just down for the day on business."

She was a solid, no-nonsense executive. I knew the type. Always in control and never letting her guard down. She was also a talented research scientist according to Dr. Abramson's list. ... charming, well-dressed, feminine, attractive, and decisive.

"I understand your work here is on longevity and the rejuvenation of human cell tissue."

"Who told you that?"

"Dr. Abramson, of course. That's why he referred me to you."

"Yes, of course. Dr. Abramson, a fine scientist. But you needn't have disguised your visit as a prospective client, Mr. Conway. I would be happy to see anyone referred by Dr. Abramson."

I smiled, a little embarrassed by the failure of my cover.

"Well, I guess I'm not the 007 type after all. I'm sorry, Dr. I wanted to get a true perspective on your work about rejuvenation. I should have been up front with you. Do you wish me to leave?" I started to stand up but she waved me back onto the couch.

"No, not at all. I only wanted to unmask you so that we could have an honest interview and not a slanted undercover story. I want you to see the real truth of my work. After all, it's a matter of record our research operates under public and government grants; only a few areas are Top Secret."

"Are you working for the government, Dr. Trent?"

"Aren't we all, Mr. Conway?"

"O.K., so I'm just asking. What can you tell me about the advances being made in longevity and cell rejuvenation?"

"Not much you don't already know from watching the Discovery and Learning channels. The real work is still out there like sunken treasures waiting to be found."

She was stonewalling me, so I thought to try the round-about approach. She was tousling the back of her long red hair behind her neck ... You know, that thing that women do so well when the curtain comes down on the conversation.

"What about the black market for human organs? What's to become of a society where the rich cannibalize the 'have-nots' for spare parts? Some clinics have been reported to be doing business with these marketers of human flesh."

"It was bound to happen, Mr. Conway. Read your history. The elite have always had their way ... and who's to stop them. Money can buy anything."

"Even immortality?" I asked.

"What would you give to live a little longer if your heart or one of your other vital organs was terminally diseased, Mr. Conway?"

"I'd hope I would want to find a donor legally."

"What if you couldn't wait? Would you buy your way up to the front of the line? Or, buy a spare part if it was offered for a price? ... not asking or wanting to know the source of the organ?"

"I couldn't deny she had a point. But, she was enjoying it a little too much and she had me on the defensive and that is a no-win position.

I stood up to gain the advantage of height. She followed suit and walked over to the bar. "Let me get you a cool drink. A little alcohol can be healthy for you on a hot day."

"I'll have a greyhound, Doctor."

She stepped behind the bar, poured the drinks ... she made herself a juice drink ... another physiological ploy.

"All the questions are loaded, Doctor. None of us knows what we will do until it happens. But I suppose you're right. Supply and Demand. It determines the market and our moral values."

She looked me straight in the eyes as I spoke. Her eyes were icy blue. They complimented her reddish hair and fair complexion. I would guess she was ... of Irish extract. She handed me the drink.

"Morals are relative to the social laws of whatever culture you live in, Mr. Conway, and most people don't want to die."

"What's the future hold beyond transplants? Cloning? For dollars? Brain transplants?"

"Your speculation is not that far fetched." she said.

"Call me, Dave, Doctor. ... You mean a Frankensteinean society of body snatchers?"

"Possibly, but our research goes far beyond that."

Now I saw an opening. She was stimulated by a subject close to her heart. "Look, Doctor, I'm knocking at the door and no one's answering. How about letting me in for a quick peek?

  She walked back over to the couch and sat down, crossing her long shapely legs. "Very well. A brief look into a medical Shangri-La. What good are transplants of vital organs after the rest of your body deteriorates. Sooner or later all the numerous body parts begin to wither like the autumn leaves. Death would be a better alternative.

"Brain transplants are too risky ... tissue rejection. Even if you could do it, chances are your old brain would soon go the way of the rest of your body parts.

"True immortality can only be obtained by the rebirth of your essence."

"My essence? Could you clarify that a little, Doctor?"

She was getting excited as she continued to enlighten me. "Yes, your essence ... your conscious self, your center of being. ... What is thought? Consciousness, awareness of self from within ... it's not the brain. It's the chemical reaction in your brain created by minute electrical energy, the genie in a bottle ...

"But what if we could let the genie out of the bottle ... and transplant to another place ... a computer ... or even another young new body?"

"Wouldn't that be a little crowded, Dr.? Two genies in one bottle?"

"No, she purred. That would not be possible unless you evicted the other genie."

"How would you do that?"

"If we can remove your essence from your body, what is left is an empty shell ... a blank mind, dry-cleaned of all essence ... a catatonic creature sitting in a corner like a rubber ball waiting for a new essence to give it the spark of life."

"It sounds even more horrible than cloning."

"Perhaps, but it has been done with mice in the maze experiments ... by injecting brain fluid from a mouse that has successfully ran the maze and then injecting it into another mouse. The injected mouse now runs the maze successfully because some memory has been transferred to its brain."

"Isn't that a big leap of science conjecture ... from a mouse to a man, Doctor?"

"Perhaps, but the secrets of life know no limitations of size ... from the most minuscule of creatures to the dinosaurs that once roamed the earth."

"And what of the human soul, Doctor?" I knew it wasn't a scientific question, but I wanted to peel away another layer of her facade to see if she was a God-fearing human being.

"I'm a scientist, Mr. Conway, not a clergyman. If there is a soul, it most certainly is part of your essence and not your stomach or any other part of your physical being. Your life force has no physical form as we know it. You look tired, Dave."

She leaned over toward me, looking into my eyes again, which, at the moment seemed unable to focus too well. I started to get up, but my legs and arms felt like soft ropes.

The glass dropped from my hand, the room grew dim, and started to tilt up to the ceiling ... or was it me on my back looking up at the ceiling. Just as the room faded into darkness, I heard Mr. Raven say, "I told you the next time you hear my voice it might be the last thing you would hear."

"Imagine yourself, an elderly diseased physical wreck, the flood waters of death rising up to engulf you ... You are doomed. Nothing can save you except your financial wealth."

CHAPTER 14

MR. RAVEN

The sunlight hurt my eyes ... I blinked my eyelids trying to block it out. I tried to see ... I couldn't seem to remember where I was in time and space ... home, waking up? No ... the beach? ... The haze started to clear as I heard a man's voice say, "He's coming out of it. Get the doctor."

Fading footsteps ... more voices. "The doctor?, I thought. Am I in a hospital? ... a car accident?...My eyes began to focus on the bright light overhead...not the sun, but a bright lamp...not the dentist... I hoped...Suddenly my memory got off the slowing merry-go-round and started putting things in order ... At first reality was a welcome relief like when you first awakc from a bad dream that seemed so real. I was in Palm Springs...The Temple of Isis.

Fiona's lovely face looked down at my own from above. The warm feeling started to turn cool as I remembered hearing Mr. Raven's voice before I melted into Dr. Trent's plush carpet that turned into quicksand. Then cool turned to ice cold as I became aware of the physical restraints on my legs, arms and midsection. I could barely move except for my head, and my hands just below the wrist. My heart started pumping like a new oil rig. I tried to speak but my mouth was too loose and dry, and my throat too tight.

Fiona lifted up my eyelids. They felt like twin unmade
beds. "Relax. The drug you took makes it difficult to
talk. It will pass in a few minutes."

"I didn't take any drug." I whispered in a hoarse voice.
"Dr. Trent drugged my drink. You've got to help me." I
turned my head to see where I was. The walls and floor
were covered in light green tiles. I tried to sit up; I couldn't
move. I lifted my head to see what was holding me down.
I was wearing a white hospital gown, laid out on a table
and strapped down. I was in a fully equipped operating
room: metal oxygen tanks, hoses, monitors, lights, a tray
filled with medical instruments the purpose of which
terrified me to think about.

I was on an operating table; I panicked and started to
struggle. I tried to shout, but it was no use. My screaming
whispers wouldn't startle a mouse. "Fiona, un-strap me!
Dr. Trent and Mr. Raven are murderers! Call the police!"

She looked at me with a sympathetic smile as she wiped
my cold sweating brow with a small towel. "Don't struggle.
There will be no pain in your rebirth. Dr. Trent will be
here shortly. Be careful," she snapped, " you will damage
the body."

"What body?" I thought, "Is there another body in the
room?" I looked around. "What the hell does she mean?
She must he tripped out on drugs." Then slowly, like a
small leak in the garden hose, the horrible thought began
to spill out!

"Tilt the table upwards for Mr. Conway's visual comfort,
Hugo!" Dr. Trent's smiling face met my upward glide.

The coke machine with the head adjusted the table and then stepped back to allow Dr. Trent to move closer to me. She lifted one of my eyelids with two long fingers.

"You are looking much better than at our last meeting this afternoon. Perhaps the spa agrees with you." She dropped my loose eyelid and began to examine the surgical tools on her tray.

"You're crazy, Dr. Trent. I'm a well known writer. People know I'm here. Now ... cut me loose! ... and we'll talk things over." It was a desperate attempt to reason with her. Perhaps she would reconsider whatever mad experiment she planned if I convinced her that my rescue was imminent. My voice was getting stronger, but my breathing was convulsive and my mouth was full of cotton balls. "Water! I need a drink!"

"Another drink, Mr. Conway? My, how daring and trusting considering the last one I gave you." She ordered the water with a wave of her hand. The sadistic bitch was enjoying the moment, and nothing short of a miracle could save me.

Fiona held my head as I sipped the water from the paper cup she held to my mouth.

Dr. Trent was wearing an operating gown. Fiona and the granite faced man from the park started to suit up. Oxygen tank hoses and medical instruments were being realigned, as well as ... electronic instruments, computer monitors, ...

Up above, a small skylight revealed a black starless square that flashed silver white every few seconds. A tall swaying palm tree peeked into the room through the high side windows.. Sudden desert thunderstorms and flash floods are a common occurrence in the 'Springs' and most institutions are prepared for it in case of an electrical power failure.

But it would be wishful thinking to hope the spa had not prepared for that likelihood. I looked around the tile room for anything ... any useful device that might be used to effect my escape. But ... my inability to move reduced that possibility to a zero. ... ... Try to stall for time, I thought. That's the only weapon you've got ... time. Sometimes your friend ... sometimes ... your enemy. Napoleon once said to his generals about time, "Ask me for anything but that."

"Dr. Trent, there is so much more I would like to know? Where is Mr. Raven? I heard his voice in your office."

"He will be here shortly. He's very anxious to meet you." she leaned into my face, "... personally." She seemed amused by the prospect and smiled as I crossed my fingers; the only physical force I could rally to my aide. "So you wish to know the answers to this complex puzzle? Very well, Mr. Conway. I suppose the old tradition of granting a dying man's last request, within limits, of course, should be indulged. We have preparations to make for the surgery, and I would like the drug I gave you to wear off. You must have many questions..

"But first, let me dash your hopes of rescue by your publisher, Mr. Chrysler. It will make you a much better listener if you are not distracted by false hopes. He phoned earlier this evening inquiring about your visit to the spa. I spoke to him myself and assured him you were here and had left for the Palm Springs Airport late this afternoon. I suggested he contact the police and try to find your car at the airport parking lot, which, by the way, is where my man parked it. He was quite appreciative. I asked him to please keep me advised. I was concerned when you were here this afternoon. You seemed to be in some kind of trouble. I would guess it would take them several days to find out if you got on one of the many flights out of the 'Springs' ... since you were probably flying under an assumed name."

My last hope was Harry. Perhaps Dr. Trent was right. I reconciled myself to my hopeless predicament for the moment. My curiosity was overwhelming.

"Now, as to your present status ... let us say that you will be in a state of limbo: neither dead or alive. You will recall my earlier explanation of immortality ... What good are vital organ transplants if your body is old and diseased ... why not escape death ... not delay it temporarily ... but to avoid it as a minor intruder into your existence.

"For the past twenty years I have successfully experimented with animals and humans in that endeavor. There were the usual glitches here and there ... deaths and mental deformities ... but overall ... well, within acceptable limits."

"What do you define as glitches and acceptable limits, Dr.?"

"Let me respond to that by asking you a question. What price in human deaths would you put on the successful conclusion of World War II? Millions would be an understatement. If Japan had won that war, we would be having this conversation in Japanese.

"Human life is so plentiful and cheap. Look at all the wasteful genocides of history. What vast scientific strides in science could have been made with such human resources."

"Are you equating genocide to scientific research?"

"No, merely the waste of human life."

"You say you've had success with this method of transferring the individual human essence from one body to another. How successful? ... or are you hiding some of your so-called glitches in the cellar?"

She laughed as her eyes glistened with excitement. "Look around this room, Dave. May I call you, Dave?"

"Sure, Helen, why not. After all, we've been through a lot together. Formalities would seem a little phony." It gave me a small lift to be able to counter punch back at her.

She liked the game we were playing and I was praying she would play with me a little longer while I continued to try to loosen the nylon straps by turning my wrist back and forth.

"Every person in this room; Fiona, Hugo, and William, your friend from the park, are ... Reborns ... Survivors ... Give it any name you like.

"Imagine yourself, an elderly diseased physical wreck, the flood waters of death rising up to engulf you ... you have no physical strength left. You are doomed. Nothing can save you except your financial wealth. Would you give it up for a second chance, or even a third? I nodded my head 'Yes'. I didn't want to make her angry; just talkative.

"You're God Damned right, you would! You can't take it with you, they say. But now, if you are willing to part with most of it, you can take some of it with you and start over to amass new wealth."

"I suspect you are overly concerned about the actual process of the procedures. It must be a little unsettling to see all these operating instruments." She picked up a scalpel from the tray of instruments and held it up to the light. She came toward me.

I drew back from the scalpel which she now held inches from my eyes. "You will feel no pain. Small incisions are made into the tissue above the skull; six minute holes are drilled through the skull ... here ... here ... here ... here ... here ... and here." She was using the scalpel as a pointer and I could feel the sharp edge as she tapped the thin skin of my scalp causing a small trickle of blood to run down one side of my head and into my ear..

She showed me a thin needle-shaped drill bit. Six micro-size holes are drilled into the skull allowing six electronic probes to be inserted into the brain." My eyes widened.

"Yes, David, into the brain to the source of electrical energy. Did you know the brain, the receiver of messages of pain from every other part of the body, is itself unable to sense pain. It has no pain receptors? Uncanny, isn't it? Think of it as a power plant; a storehouse of power. That is your brain's electrical energy ... your essence.

"The six probes will transmit the electrical impulses of the brain to a computer where it will be downloaded into data and stored for uploading and retransmission into another brain, where the chemical process reconstructs the data, leaving your brain like an empty coconut shell.

"However, we won't be retransmitting your essence. Of course I'm oversimplifying the process." She moved away from me much to my relief, and continued her preparations ... and her explanations. She was proud of her work.

"The recovery period for a client is only twenty-four hours. The procedure leaves no visible scars. The only difficulty is in learning to physically coordinate their movements and functions of the new body. One's perception of the past physical world does not translate to the new body.

"Several days at the clinic are required for therapy and orientation. Perception of distances are a particular problem, but after a time, like a newborn child, physical coordination improves dramatically." She wheeled the electronic equipment closer to the table. "Thereafter, annual checkups and some medication are required to maintain the body's homeostasis".

She saw the puzzled look in my face. " ... Equilibrium ... stability! David. Like a gyro keeping your senses in proper balance."

I had to keep her talking. "You said everybody in this room ... is a reborn? What about you, Helen?"

She looked at me with a piercing laser glare that would penetrate a steel plate. "I have not yet found it necessary to take the journey of rebirth.

"Fiona has shown you what a little surgery and hormone treatment can do for our regular clients. Now add to that some unorthodox rejuvenating methods, such as: gland and skin transplants ... drugs .... I'm a lot older than you think, Dave. And, of course, I have to lie a little about my age ... and be careful not to have friends who want to know my beauty secrets."

"How old, Helen? Fifty? Sixty?"

She kept shaking her head in the negative. "A woman doesn't like to tell her age, but pride in my work takes precedence over feminine vanity.   I was born in 1918." My mind did the arithmetic. Her appearance said the arithmetic lied.

"Perhaps I'll try being a man in my rebirth; the opportunities of this discovery are endless ... and very titillating." She smiled, her eyes were half closed.

Suddenly she snapped out of her thoughts and got back to the business at hand ... sucking my mind dry.

She continued her preparations for the operation as she spoke; checking monitors, making notes. The others were also occupied in their preparations as well.

I kept moving my sweating wrists; slowly twisting them to lubricate and put a strain on the nylon straps. "And what about the people whose bodies you hi-jack? Won't they be missed?"

She was amused by my obvious questions. "A little plastic surgery to alter features and new identities; all are easily arranged. But the best method is to use bodies from a different country. You, for instance, will be a German. Our client is a 75-year old industrialist worth billions. He would like to be about 35-years old again, and in excellent health. We have already done a total blood and physical scan of your body. You're in excellent condition. Your voice will be speaking in German by tomorrow and your true identity will be easily overlooked. Arrangements have been made to transfer power and money to the client's new identity."

"How do they know they can trust you?

"They can trust us for two reasons: It's a referral business that depends on client satisfaction. And, most important ... they have no choice. We are the last off ramp on the Expressway to the cemetery."

"And what about my essence? Where will you store it?"

"I'm afraid we're not in the storage business ... yet. But that will be forthcoming in the near future. Your essence has little value unless you can pay the fee. And even if you could, your boy scout mentality would be bound to hunt me down. I'm afraid we'll just have to do with you what we do with all rejects. Your digitized essence will be deleted ... erased."

The thought was revolting, but time was working for me, so I continued. "A sad ending for a writer, but not unusual. Still, I have many more questions."

"Of course you do, but we do have a schedule to maintain, so be brief."

"Dr. Abramson? Is he part of your organization? Is he Mr. Raven?"

"No. Your visit to him was a lucky coincidence. As for Mr. Raven, let me introduce you to him."

She reached into a pocket under her gown and took out a square credit card size device about an inch thick. She held it up to her mouth and spoke.

"We meet at last, Mr. Conway." said the voice of Mr. Raven. She had used a voice synthesizer. "This device can lower or raise the frequency of my voice." Her voice sounded like a baritone and then a soprano.

"You're alone in this madness?"

"Not quite. At times I had partners, but necessity required a complete dissolution of same by death ... for security purposes."

"You murdered them?"

"I reassigned them! David, you're just not corporate-minded. The bottomline dictates decisions. Your next question will undoubtedly be, 'How did I find out about the diary, and where is Victor Monroe?' Am I correct?"

"I think I have a general idea, but I would like to hear the specifics from you, Doctor ... I mean, Helen." The lights in the operating room flickered ever so slightly. The thunderstorm outside grew in intensity. She looked up at the skylight, and said to the others.

"Don't concern yourselves. If we have a power failure, the low level emergency lights will activate immediately and the emergency generator will be activated approximately thirty seconds after that, giving us full power to continue." My heart sank.

Her incredible arrogance was driving her to unload more than she wanted me to know. But her need to boast about her incredible achievements, and her confidence that everything she told me would be deleted with the rest of my essence, relaxed her caution....

She was right, of course. She had all the cards, and she was holding a Royal Flush; I had duces, and all the chips were on the table. My father once told me, "Son. When you're in that position, there's only one thing left to do."

"What's that, Dad?"

"Kick the table over!!" I kept moving and twisting my wrists.

"Can you tell me about Col. Moran? Apparently he escaped at the Reichenbach Falls and was never caught by the authorities."

She seemed to drift into her own thoughts at the mention of Moran's name. She raised her eyes and tilted her head upward as a sardonic smile curled in the corners of her mouth. She turned full around the room and suddenly snapped back at me. "Can I tell you about Col. Moran?

Oh! Yes! Yes! I can tell you all about him ... and what
became of him." That sardonic smile quickly turned into
a sneer as she said, "He was my adoptive father. He
brought me up to study biology in the hope that I could
assist and further the experiment that Prof. Moriarty and
Dr. Kosnov had started." This revelation of Col. Moran
and Dr. Trent conspiring together only increased my fear
of this deadly situation. The immensity of it all was too much.

She continued to speak and I continued to sweat. She
walked the room gesturing to the pale green walls as she
continued her story. The thunder and lighting added to the
intensity of the moment. She was possessed with the
passion of the retelling. ... The tile walls mirrored each
lightning flash. The lights grew dimmer and the room
glowed in an eerie green light.

"I will tell you about Col. Moran . I was born in 1918 in
New York City. I knew nothing of my parents, and was
sent to an orphanage where I stayed until I was five years
old. Col. Moran and his mistress of the moment raised me
as their own. He would never marry and was too much
into his own existence to share it with another except for
my adoption.

"Years later, when I asked him about this inconsistency in
his nature, he would explain he wanted someone close that
he could train to work with him as a medical colleague in
the field of biology. So, he would educate and train me to
become a medical doctor specializing in that field of
medicine. I never knew his real name wasn't Trent until
years later.

"Col. Moran was not a young man when he adopted me.
His age was 67. Yet, due to experiments by his medical
partner and his own medical knowledge, they were able to
keep his youth and vigor in bloom at least 25 years beyond
their expected decline. His appearance was not much

changed since the incident at the Reichenbach Falls in the year of 1888.

"He appeared middle-aged ... in his mid forties. He was a vain man with an enormous ego. Naturally he would keep a written account of his exploits which I came upon much later and learned about the man; writer, hunter, murderer, card cheat, mercenary, thief, solder, ... all were among his many talents.

"I will recount to you from his writings, only that part of his life that has brought us all to this moment and place in time." She looked deep into my eyes as she left the present, taking my mind with hers into the dark past.

"I have hunted lions, tigers, cannibals, and pirates ... man or beast ... I do not fear ... least of all your rich and powerful friends."

CHAPTER 15

THE ESCAPE FROM REICHENBACH FALLS

I looked down at the tumbling avalanche of ice and snow ... descending upon the castle and now overtaking the carriage containing Moriarty, Dr. Kosnov, and Holmes. I was elated with the prospect of being rid of them all at one time, and if that blasted Dr. Watson doesn't escape the cascade of death, then no one will be left alive to tell the tale.

My view of the victims was totally obscured just seconds before the onslaught of the mountain. I waited for the mountain to cease its breathing, but it was of no use. One small rumble would follow another, creating more white fog. Nothing could have survived the avalanche caused by the explosive charges I set off prematurely. I laughed at the thought of Moriarty being outsmarted by his own stupidity. I had to get back to London where the duplicate documents I had made of Dr. Kosnov's experiment notes were hidden. Did that arrogant egomaniac Moriarty think I would serve only his attempt at immortality.

I rode the horse I had stolen from Dr. Watson over rugged mountain trails to a small obscure hamlet where I rested for several days to collect my thoughts and make plans for the continuation of the experiments. There remained only the job of finding a none-to-reputable medical doctor who would gladly join me in the quest for extended life.

The next two years found me on the run from the police. England was too dangerous for me thanks to the survival of Dr. Watson at the Falls and the letters sent by Holmes to Scotland Yard. Well, at least Holmes was dead. I won't have to worry about having that crafty devil on my trail. At least, that is what I thought at the time.

It was not until three years after Reichenbach Falls that I found out he was still alive, therefore he must have continued his investigations of Moriarty's replicas.

I had stayed clear of that element of the experiment as it would be of no use in my attempts at longevity. As luck would have it, I fell through the cracks in the floor boards of Holmes' investigation. I had left England one year before his return. Language was not my best subject, beyond Swahili used in the jungle on the hunt. I would have to have false papers if I were to immigrate to an English-speaking country. Perhaps Australia, or America ... the Land of Opportunity.

The choice was obvious ... America. Opportunity is my business. Unfortunately, I took the name of Victor Monroe, one of the replicas that died at birth. It was easy to change dates on the Birth Certificate; a little aging to the document was done with tea and sunlight. Had I known Holmes had survived, I would have taken another name. Dr. Watson would be sure to chronicle the story of the 'Ripper'.

I would have to be on guard in America and change my identity as quickly as possible. Holmes would be sure to be on my trail ... if he made a connection. But as I said, 'I seem to have fallen through the cracks.' Now was the right time to find a medical man.

In 1891 the New York City police force had hired many Irish immigrants, and being Irish, I had little trouble finding a fellow Irishman on the force to arrange an appointment for me to apply for a job with his chief.

My military training impressed him. Of course, in those days a man's past was difficult to investigate. I used the name Trent; I was hired immediately.

The New York City police force was an ideal place to hang my hat; graft and political corruption were flourishing like wild flowers and I would be one of its many gardeners. I made connections with the right people and lined my pockets. In four years I made Detective, First Grade. I knew more about crime than the criminals I arrested. The abhorrent stupidity of the blundering bastards was incredible.

In the year of 1895, I had come upon an illegal abortionist who was quite wealthy. He served only the most elite of clients.

I could see at once there was a little extra money to be made from those little darlings of the rich and powerful who required a doctor's discreet medical services. Their wives and daughters were a lustful lot, and the men had many mistresses to maintain in pristine physical condition.

I made my plan to enlist him into my service and would leave him no exit by which to renege on any agreement. I came upon him late one rainy night in October outside his fashionable brownstone off Park Avenue.

He was with an elegant lady. She was dressed in furs and jewels. I had paid the head waiter at Delmonicos Restaurant to send word to me when they left for his residence where he would, no doubt, continue the debauchery of the lady.

Their carriage arrived and they were about to dismiss the driver when I interrupted the woman's exit from the carriage by standing in front of her..

"Good evening, Dr. Frazer. I believe we have an appointment?" They were taken off guard, of course, and the lady's distress was apparent. I let the doctor step down onto the sidewalk.

"Do I know you, Sir? What is the meaning of this intrusion at this late hour?"

"We have urgent business to discuss, Dr."

"My office hours are during the day. You may drop around at an appropriate hour to make an appointment for whatever ails you, although I suspect it will be more a mental disorder than a physical one. Now be off before I have the cabby call for the police." He turned and was about to instruct the coachman to do just that as I placed my Detective Badge in front of his face.

"'Since I am the police, that will not be necessary. " I turned to the woman. "The hour is late, Miss, and you must get your beauty rest." I took her by the arm and placed her back into her seat, giving the driver a fiver to take the lady home. She opened her mouth to speak, but I put my finger to her lips; she knew not to talk. The driver snapped the horses into motion as Dr. Frazer came forward to protest my actions.

I struck him across the face with the back of my hand causing him to fall backward and to bleed heavily from the nose. "Now let us go inside Dr. and talk about our future arrangements." I took him by the elbow and walked him to the front door. We entered the brownstone and went directly to his study. He sat down as I poured the drinks while he tended to his bruised nose.

He was in his mid thirties, medium build, hair thinning on the top, and very much a peacock of a man, strutting about town to attract the ladies' attentions, no doubt.

The study was overly masculine, indicating a gnawing insecurity and the need to demonstrate his manhood. He was a Mama's Boy ... a pansy. He continued to protest. "'I know powerful people. The will come to my aid. I will have your badge, Detective..."

"Trent. Detective Trent."

"Get out of my house! I will call the servants." He started to stand up.

"It's their night off. Sit still!" I shoved him back into his chair. "... Now listen to me, you milque toast bunny. I have hunted lions, tigers, cannibals, and pirates ... man or beast ... I do not fear ... least of all your rich and powerful friends. You are just a slimy abortionist to these people. They use you like a doormat to wipe their feet.

"I know everything about you. You gamble badly ... you owe money ...you drink heavily ... and you like the ladies ... and a boy from time to time." He started to speak, but my loud voice silenced him. "The rich won't have you as a guest in their homes. They just tip you good to keep your tongue from wagging. You are nothing but a trained monkey; a dog doing parlor tricks for a bone." I handed him his drink and stood above him.

He started to rise up from his chair in protest, but he saw it in my eyes ... that truth no man wants to see in the eyes of another. He sat back into his chair like the beaten dog he was and drank the glass dry. I stood over him as I spoke.

"Doctor, a door of enormous opportunity is about to open for you. Do as I say, and you will be rich, respected, and have the women of the world to choose from, and more ... much more. Deny me and I will see to it that you are a dead man within the hour, and by the will of your rich friends to boot ... who will thank me for stilling your voice."

He was both excited and confused. I had offered him his heart's desire and all that he had dreamed. "The devil could not make you a better offer, and you don't have to give up your soul, for I am sure it was lost long ago." I took him by the collar. "I could hold you to me by fear, but I want you beholden to me by greed." He signed up like a peachfuzz recruit, for he knew I could do as I promised. My will is strong and he was no match for it.

He looked up and said, "I believe you. I am at your service."

In the months that followed, I took over the discreet management of the doctor's practice. We opened a private hospital.

At first, the powerful and wealthy approved of the new arrangement as it would double their sense of security. I advised them that such increased discretion would also double the price, not only in cash, but in other business opportunities. They would provide inside information on stocks and business ventures as well. Further, we would tolerate no interlopers into the field as our files were quite extensive and our operating cost escalating by the hour.

Contributions to our monthly maintenance cost would further our loyalty. We no longer would accept the slim pickings of the hunt on the fringe area of the kill like wild dogs and jackals. We must be welcome to feed among the eaters at the main table.

And so all that I had promised Dr. Frazer, was a reality come true. Soon he would marry into one of the '100' families of New York City. I resigned from the police force as money was no longer a problem.

He is ready, I thought, to bring him into the next chapter of my plan; the continuation of the experiment. I told him just enough to whet his appetite. And what an appetite it was! His greed knew no bounds. I knew I could trust a man with a vice of such enormity.

NEW YORK CITY ... 1920

It had been almost 25 years since I had enlisted the aid of Dr. Frazer into my plan. I had told him only what he needed to know. He never found out about England or Moriarty. If he had I would almost certainly have dispatched his earthly existence to the next life.

We had achieved some successful rejuvenation results on our own persons ... the duplication of three replicas of myself met with some success and their expected full blossom into manhood would be in 1942.

However, one of the three was defective ... unusable.

We had determined from experiments that the maturity of the vital organs and glands are necessary if the best results are to be achieved.

The replicas would be at optimum maturity in their early twenties.

And so we continued to hold back the ravages of time at approximately a one and a half to one ratio; one and a half years of aging for every two. Extremely encouraging.

A twenty-five percent increase in the life expectancy of an aging man translates into an additional twenty years of youthful vitality. But, we would need to decrease the rate of aging for us by one year for every two, as I was already well into middle-age.

I could wait for the replicas to mature. I would still be a fairly active man appearing to be in my sixties when in reality I would be over ninety years old.

I trained Helen for one purpose, and one purpose only; to replace Dr. Frazer, who was becoming a bit too ambitious and would surely become an outdated liability in the course of the next 15 years.. Helen had great talent. It was evident in her childhood. The adoption center had advised me of her skills.

1940

In 1940 world war appeared to be evident. Our research had bogged down on several points. The main one being to keep the human organs from degrading once removed from the body of the so-called donor.

Refrigeration helped but it also caused more problems; crystallization of the blood and tissue. I was frustrated with the lack of progress by Dr. Frazer who, although ten years my junior, was deteriorating at an alarming rate. His lusty indulgence caused his body to extract a price from the extra time he had been given.

It was then that Helen made the breakthrough; the correct drug to prevent the crystallization of blood and tissue. I had accelerated her education years before. She was only twenty-two and a medical doctor just completing her internship at our clinic where I was Chief Administrator. Naturally she had received special training and considerations by the best physicians.

Helen proved to be as willing as I to unlock the secrets of life, even if it meant using unorthodox methods ... I told her of the two replicas.

Many of our reluctant patient volunteers assisted in the experiments. When one went wrong, we classified it as a death by natural causes. We were never questioned; our credentials were impeccable.

It was time to give Dr. Frazer notice that his services were no longer required on this earth. He knew too much and had become too demanding. I suppose I felt a twinge of sentimentality toward the old fool; after all, we had been partners for almost 36 years. So I did what must be done in a humane manner.

I invited him late one evening into my office for a drink and the prospect of a lascivious evening with two young nurses from the hospital staff. We sat in the two leather lounge chairs sipping brandy beside the fireplace which glowed red with burning logs on that chilly night. The bottle was on a small table between our chairs. I leaned toward him as I spoke.

"We have come a long way together on this journey, or should I say quest. Yes, quest! It would be, by God! A quest for the most valuable treasure of all time ... Immortality!! Better than all the gold in the world. Aye, and all the time in the world to spend all the gold in the world." We both laughed. His laughter faded into a vulgar leer as he asked.

"Where are the young ladies, Mr. Trent? Should not our clandestine celebration include them as well? After all, two lusty men like ourselves shouldn't be without the comfort of a woman's arms." He was already a little drunk, having had a few drinks before he came to my office.

Suddenly his mood got dark, as I knew it would from previous drinking episodes. Liquor would loosen his tongue and give him courage to say things he would never dare to say to me if he were sober. And tonight, he was full of liquor courage.

"You know, Trent, I have contributed all the medical skill and knowledge to this 'quest' as you call it, yet I have no replacement replicas of my own. You have immortality within reach; I have nothing!" He stood up and flung his glass into the fireplace. "I need to know I have a chance to survive. You can't deny me any longer by fear. I stood up. He backed away.

"I have kept my promises to you, Doctor ... wealth, power, women, position, respect ..."

"Yes, but you promised me eternal life as well."

I moved closer. "You shall have it, Doctor; the eternal life as promised in the Bible. And, it can only be obtained by leaving your earthly bonds behind." I moved toward him. His liquor courage spilled out of his trousers as his bladder let go from fear. He started to whimper and shake. He was like a small animal waiting for the tiger to pounce upon him.

I took him by the throat with one hand and took out the hypodermic needle with the other. I injected him in the neck with a paralyzing drug that would give the appearance of death. He went into a coma-like state that caused his facial features to swell beyond recognition.

The next morning I gave the unsuspecting student interns a fresh cadaver to open up and study. They were a clumsy lot and not too meticulous about their work; they did not detect his almost imperceptible pulse.

1941

In 1941, I was 91 years old and beginning to show signs of an advanced heart condition as well as liver failure. If I were to survive I would have to have transplants immediately.

My appearance and physical condition was that of a man in his mid-sixties. The operation posed no great threat.

However, World War II had begun and two of the replicas were now in uniform and in the thick of it in the South Pacific and North Africa.

We had kept careful track of them all their lives; both were born in America; one in the Midwest and one in the East. Both were excellent physical specimens as far as we could determine from afar. Our only contact had been through paid observers living near both families who adopted the children and raised them as their own.

The observers, local medical doctors, were only advised that we were conducting scientific studies of child growth to adulthood ... other children were included in the study so as not to arouse the suspicion of the medical doctors sending reports to our clinic at regular one-year intervals.

Most Americans felt war was imminent, but we did not anticipate the suddenness of it as a result of the Japanese attack at Pearl Harbor on December 7, 1941. The country was galvanized into action. All differences of opinion vanished instantly. Americans were of one mind with one thought: Avenge the Japanese attack on Pearl Harbor that took the lives of several thousand civilians and Navy personnel.

Young men waited outside recruiting stations to join up the following morning. Others were drafted in a matter of days. The military was mobilizing at an incredible velocity.

The two replicas were out of our reach for the moment. We had hoped to abduct one or both at the earliest opportunity. Unfortunately, they were among the many early casualties of the war.

I knew I would be a dead man in less than a year unless I utilized my only other alternative. It would not be easy and I had hoped it would not come to this. I would have to transplant the vital organs of the remaining defective replica ... into my body.

The sounds of thunder filling the operating room were deafening. It seemed to shake Dr. Trent out of her intense state of thought, but she then returned to relating her story. "Those were the last written words he ever sat down on paper."

I could see it in her eyes ... her hate for the man was intensive. I didn't want her to compose herself too quickly, so I kept at her with more questions.

"What happened to Moran?" She slowly turned and came toward me with a scalpel in her hand. I kept twisting my wrists. The nylon straps were soaked with sweat and blood. Blood was a good lubricant. She stopped, standing very close to me as she adjusted the table to a flat position. She leaned over me and said, "It is almost time, David ..."

My mind was in a frenzy of thoughts. My body was ridged with fright. I yelled out to her. "Wait! Wait!" I turned my head to avoid the scalpel. She grabbed my jaw ... turning my head to face her.

"Not yet, David. Not yet. Just a few more minutes. Bring over the head restraint." Hugo wheeled over a small metal table upon which was constructed a steel head post with screw clamps and straps.

"Tell me about Moran." I shouted. She stood silent, staring at me and yet looking beyond me or through me to a past event.

She turned, staring at the raging storm outside the rattling window glass. She put the scalpel down on the tray and walked to the window. She touched the glass with her finger tips and started to speak again about the past.

1942

I had been working late that stormy night in November 1942. The hospital staff was limited to three nurses, two orderlies, and two physicians. I had been studying the notes of all the experiments that Dr. Frazer and my father had accumulated over their years together. I couldn't find the beginning notes of their experiments. It puzzled me. It was as if one had started a book with the first chapter missing.

I decided to search the offices of my father, and the former offices of Dr. Frazer who mysteriously disappeared two years before. My efforts were unsuccessful. I had looked everywhere ... even at our Manhatten brownstone home that I shared with my father.

My previous efforts to get him to tell me more about his life and the experiment were fruitless. He would only say, "You know everything you need to know, Helen." I said nothing further to him, for I knew there was much more to learn and I needed to know it all.

He would have a written account ... somewhere. I had often seen him writing in his office late at night. I went to his office on the top floor of the hospital. The windswept rain pelted the glass windows as if tapping to be let inside. I knew how he thought. He was a clever bastard ... cold, abrupt ... harsh, and without a loving bone in his body. Our relationship was one of total indifference except where our research into longevity was concerned.

The nature of his vanity would compel him to keep a record of his exploits. ... He would have a hidden record in a secret place ... perhaps his desk. I decided to examine it thoroughly. I pulled out several of the drawers and used an extra key I had, to unlock the middle top drawer. Nothing was apparent. I had seen him write in a large bound book ... similar to a ledger book. I stood back from the desk to view it as a whole.

The sound of the rain grew louder. I looked out the window, then turned back to the desk. That's when I noticed I hadn't pulled one drawer out far enough. It protruded only one-half the distance of the ones above it. I knelt down to inspect the rear section of the drawer. I tried to pull it out further, but it wouldn't move. I could see the rear panel of the drawer. It was out as far as it would go.

The conclusion was obvious. There had to be a secret compartment behind the rear of the drawer. I found it under the left rear of the desk. A spring latch hidden in the underside of the desk released a panel that opened revealing a large ledger book.

I spent the night reading the book. It was dawn when I finished. As he had said, I knew everything there was to know,...and now I knew...what he did not want me to know!

The next few days I was careful to be my usual self, especially around him. And then it came ... the moment I had both feared and expected.

He called me into his office that afternoon and said he wanted me to come to his office late in the evening to meet with one of the older physicians whom I knew to be a surgeon. He said he had enlisted this new surgeon into our research and he wanted to discuss the details in private after hours.

That night I arrived at his office at 9 PM, the expected hour of our meeting. They were both there waiting. We made some small talk about the clinic and then he made his move. He walked over to the bar and poured three drinks.

"This is a very special occasion, Helen. Dr. Steiger has agreed to join us in our research; I have given him only a brief overview.

"Although you are young, I think your incredible abilities, along with Dr. Steiger's experience, will accelerate our research." He gave us each a glass of Irish whiskey. He had taught me to drink it when I was quite young. He raised his glass. Dr. Steiger and I raised ours. They drank; I didn't!

"What's wrong, Helen? Why aren't you drinking?

"I've decided to quit drinking. It could be bad for my liver … or heart." His eyes grew shiny and fierce.

"Nonsense, Helen. Drink up. It's a special occasion." He sat down behind his desk. It was not a request. It was an order. Dr. Steiger was becoming a little nervous. His fingers kept tapping the glass he held in his other hand. I stood up.

"I think not, Father!"

"Drink the goddamn drink!" he yelled as he stood up from his chair, "or I'll shove it down your throat!" He came at me only to see the barrel of a .38 revolver shoved under his chin; the same gun he had taught me to shoot years before.

"Move back, Moran!" My words struck him dumb. He backed away ... to his desk and sat back in his chair.

"So you have read my notes? All right! We'll make other arrangements. We can start over. He reached toward one of the drawers in his desk.

"The gun you keep in that drawer is not there."

Dr. Steiger stood up and started for the door.

"I think I should leave." he said.

"Sit down, Doctor. My fath......" I couldn't say the word. "... Moran will tell you I'm an excellent shot." The doctor did as he was told.

"Don't listen to her, Steiger. She's bluffing. She can't handle us both."

"I won't have to. Have you noticed you are both sweating? I came to your office after you left today. I took your revolver and laced your whiskey with a paralytic drug.

"The same drug you slipped into the glass you were expecting me to drink.

It's effects are quite sudden. First, your eyes lose focus ... then your speech becomes slurred and your legs melt out from under you. Your arms and hands hang like curtains. They were both in that stage; barely able to talk, but conscious and hearing everything I said. Moran tried to stand up. His mumbled words fell out of his drooling mouth.

"Helen, I made a mistake. I ... don't ..." He fell back into the chair.

"I'm going to kill you, Moran. You were going to transplant vital organs from my body into yours. I'm the third replica; the one that didn't quite replicate the same as the other two ... the defective one.

"Your vanity compelled you to adopt me. What could be better than a partnership with yourself. You could groom me to become what you wanted me to be. You knew my limitations. I'm almost identical to you in every way ... even the survival instinct is the same." I walked toward the desk.

"Do I see fear in your eyes?" I leaned over the desk, looking into his face. "Yes! It's there! I see it deep in the pools of your eyes, little sparks of flashing light. Fear! You never knew it before; not with tigers or men ... but, you never had to face yourself, Moran. You are going to be killed by your other self." He could only sit there drooling as his eyes cried out for mercy.

Dr. Steiger was in an even worse state. I stood over him. I took a large hypodermic needle from my coat pocket already filled with serum. The doctors eyes rained tears.

I injected him in the neck ... directly into the artery. "Listen, Dr. Steiger, and you may live a little longer. I have given you an injection to counteract the paralytic drug. You will be able to move in a few moments. You will help me walk Moran to the nearby Subway Station. If you don't I will shoot you. I also know about several of your incompetent surgeries that have resulted in one patient's death and the lifelong deformity of another. I'll ruin your medical career if you try to escape. Join me, and you may drink from the fountain of youth."

It was about 10 PM when we arrived at the Subway Station. Moran was barely able to walk. We moved him like a stumbling drunk. We managed to get down to the end of the platform where the train would come into the station. Only one or two people were on the platform ... at the far opposite end. They were reading newspapers.

Dr. Steiger was holding Moran up as he babbled, "I can't go through with this! Do you have to do it this way? It's horrible!"

"It has to look like an accident. Shut up and do as you're told." I put the gun to his forehead. Moran was aware of what was happening. His eyes widened as the small dot of light started to emerge from the long tube of blackness.

The light grew larger, swelling like a balloon. I could see the reflection in his eyes. "Listen to the roar of the train, Moran, ... or is it the roar of a raging animal ... perhaps a tiger." I took his jaw in one hand and turned it toward the charging beast.

We began to feel the rumbling vibrations of the platform as the rails below took on the silver glow of the train's oncoming lights. Moran's eyes were screaming ... his mouth hung open like a torn pocket. He wanted to scream.

For a slight fraction of a second he regained enough strength from the emotional surge of adrenaline to his body to yell out a gurgling sound ... It sounded like the word 'Hell!' We shoved him off the platform onto the tracks to be mangled by the steel teeth of the train which rolled over him like an ocean wave.

"It is too late, Dave. There's a lot of money involved …
Your time is up."

CHAPTER 16

THE STORM ... THE PRESENT

The storm's intensity increased. The winds shook the walls and the window glass rattled almost to the breaking point. The noise was distraction enough to cause Dr. Trent and her people to pay less attention to me.

I could almost slip my right hand from the nylon strap that was soaked through with sweat and blood. One more tug would do it, but then what could I do with one free arm while the rest of my body was restrained. Dr. Trent turned her attention back to me.

"That's quite a story, Helen. What happened to Dr. Steiger?"

"I continued to work with him until his services were no longer required." She started toward me. "I terminated him."

"You mean he was reassigned?" She was going to do it now. This was it. "Look, Helen ... Dr. Trent. It's not too late to stop! You've made fantastic discoveries. The medical communities and the government would forgive all and welcome you with open arms. Think about it for a moment."

"It's too late, Dave. There's a lot of money involved and I haven't been completely candid with you. I'm out of time. Years ago I experimented with radioactive materials as part of my research. I have a terminal form of leukemia. I'll be dead in six months if I'm not reborn. I'm in no position to go through government channels. Your time is up." She motioned to the others to get started.

This was it! All or nothing! I started to pull my arm loose. The building shook as a massive bolt of lightning struck the top of a palm tree outside. The lights flickered ... then went out. I pulled my arm loose, and in the confusion I was able to unbuckle the straps on my left arm as well. ... then the chest restraint.

The red emergency light came on. I reached over for the tray of instruments. I snatched a large cutting tool from the tray and cut the straps off my legs as Hugo and William came at me like a pair of junkyard dogs.

I rolled off the table toward Dr. Trent. I still had the surgical knife in my hand. I spun her around and pulled her up against me, and put her in a strangle-hold ... I held the knife against her neck.

The dogs stopped as Dr. Trent put her hands up to halt them. Just then the emergency generators kicked in and the room lights came back on.

"Move over to the side wall, you bastards! You, too, Fiona! I've got nothing to lose. ... Move!" I shouted. They jumped.

"What should we do, Dr. Trent?" they yelled back.

"Nothing. Let him alone. He won't kill his shield."

"I will, if I don't get out of here. How does it feel, Bitch, to have a knife at your throat for a change?" I pulled her back with me toward the door. "Where are my clothes?"

Fiona went to a locker in the corner of the room and took my clothing from the hanger. She brought them to me. "Fiona. You're coming with me and Dr. Trent. Hugo and William! Stay!

"Don't come through these doors for ten minutes or your lifeline, ... Dr. Trent, is history." They grumbled and stood back. We went through the door into the dark hallway. Small emergency lighting made it possible to see.

"Fiona, I want car keys! ... any keys! ... now!! Let's go." We shuffled down the hallway. I let go of Dr. Trent's throat and threw her to the floor. I dressed. Then I pulled her to her feet and continued dragging her down the hallway to her office. I had the knife up against the base of her spine.

"Where are your car keys?" She pointed to the desk. "Fiona, pick them up and hand them to me. O.K., let's go! ... to your car. She turned to go out of her office.

"Not through the main entrance, Doctor. I'm sure you have a private entrance where you park your car." She pointed to a door behind the bar. We went through it into a small hallway. At the end was another door leading to the rear parking lot.

"Hold it right there. Fiona, check the door. If I see your men on the other side of that door, Doctor, I'll stick this knife right through your spinal cord. I pressed it into her back. She flinched and arched her back, as she said.

"Perhaps I was impulsive about using your body, Dave. I can see now you are a very resourceful man of action. I could use someone like you in my organization."

"No, thanks, Doc. I don't like the way you terminate partnerships. Now ... let's all move outside." The heavy downpour and a lack of parking lot lights made it difficult to see. I would have to be careful, the emergency power was for the operating room only.

We walked toward a Ford Explorer. I thought, 'a Rolls would be the car for her, but I guess utility vehicles are the 'in' thing.' I unlocked the door, still holding Dr. Trent by the wrist. I reached in to put the keys into the ignition to start it up. The engine roared and I pulled the headlight switch to on ... just in time to see Hugo and William coming around the front of the car to jump me.

I threw Dr. Trent into their path and then pushed Fiona into her, for an extra point. They all fell to the ground as I leaped into the Explorer. I put it in gear with my driver's door still open.

Hugo came up at me and I kicked him back with my left foot. He fell back to the pavement. I shut the door and drove off only to find I was heading for a 'dead end' and into the hillside that loomed up before me. I turned the wheel full circle to avoid a collision. The car stalled.

I could see Hugo and William running toward me in the headlights. I turned the ignition key, the engine just whirred and wouldn't turn over. I held the gas pedal down to the floor for a few seconds, then turned the ignition key without depressing the gas pedal. It worked! The engine started up as Hugo and William reached for my driver's door.

I put it in gear, speeding away from Hugo who hung on to the bumper for about ten yards before he let go. I drove past a very wet Dr. Trent and Fiona still wearing their operating room gowns.

There's only one main road back to LA. Would she call the police and report the car stolen? No. Too risky. But I didn't intend to go back to LA.

Harry had a lakeside cabin up in the mountains East of LA; Big Bear. That's where I'll go to sort things out. I've got to write this story and I have to contact Harry. Must be a cellular phone in this car. There it is. Right between the seats and lit up like a neon sign.

I dialed the number, but the phone wouldn't let me make a call without knowing the security code numbers. I decided to forget the phone. I couldn't take a chance on stopping at a payphone, either. They might be following me, besides all power was out.

The speedometer showed 70 MPH. A little dangerous for this kind of weather. The rain pelted the windshield without a let-up. The wipers were working at high speed and it was difficult to see beyond my headlights through the slanted curtain of rain. The cell phone rang. I suspected it would be Dr. Trent, calling to convince me to surrender. I let it ring a few more times before I picked up the receiver and heard a man's voice.

"We're right behind you, Conway. Pull over or we'll shove you off the road." I looked in the rear view mirror. It was Hugo and William flashing their headlights as they tailgated me up the mountain grade toward San Bernadino. I pressed down on the accelerator. They kept coming.

"Pull over, Conway. We've got a gun. Remember the car accident in London?" I hung up the phone.

They came alongside me. We were going 80. William extended his arm out of the passenger window holding a gun at my driver's side window. The rain smashed into his face. I hit the brakes.

They went past me and so did a Highway Patrol car with it's red lights flashing. I could see the taillights of the two cars racing into the storm. Then, in the distance a small orange fireball erupted and started rolling down the mountain to the desert floor below.

I drove on by the flashing lights of the police car which had parked on the side of the road. The deputies were standing on the edge of the drop-off looking down at the fire. I kept on driving, not trusting my first impulse to pull over and tell the whole story.

I drove through Redlands just south of San Bernadino, and up to Big Bear Lake, high in the mountains. The storm was starting to let up. In the distance the sky filled with silent flashes of white light and low rumbling sounds of thunder.

The headlights snaked through the winding mountain road casting moving shadows of the pine trees that seemed to reach out for me as the car passed. My heart started to race. The fear inside me was multiplying like pennies in a dish. I almost lost control of the wheel as it slipped through my sweating hands.

A tree jumped out into the road ... or was it a deer ... I pushed the brake pedal to the floor. stopping inches short of a hanging tree limb and the drop-off into the darkness below. My breathing was becoming more difficult; I was hyperventilating.

I cupped my hands and covered my mouth and nose, breathing slowly and deeply. After a moment or two my breathing returned to normal and my heart slowed down. I put the Explorer in reverse and backed onto the road. Then I put it into the forward gear and continued up the mountain, leaving my fears behind in the blackness.

I tried to call Harry from a pay phone in the village at Big Bear, but the storm had caused power outages there too. Harry's keys to the cabin were left, where else, under the door mat. Why doesn't he just leave the front door unlocked, I thought.

I had to settle for burning logs in the fireplace and writing by a kerosene lamp. Harry and I kept plenty of writing material at the cabin. We used to come up to fish and write.

I knew I wouldn't, and couldn't sleep, ... until I wrote this story which I would mail to Lorraine in Washington for safekeeping. I wrote all through the night and into the dawn ... now rising above the mountain tops.

That's the story. All of it up to last night. I don't know the ending yet. But I do know mankind is going to have to face a lot of difficult choices in the near future, and the medical community is going to have a lot to answer for if it allows the laws of man and nature to be manipulated by the highest bidder.

"Do you know what is better than life insurance, Dave?
AfterLife insurance!"

BIG BEAR

Even though it was summer, the mountain air was crisp with the morning chill. Dave had not slept except for a short doze and his eyes were filled with gritty sleep. He awoke just after 7 AM.

The kerosene lamp on the desk was low but still lit. In the fireplace was a smoking pile of flameless sticks ... the remnants of the three logs he had fired up last night. He walked to the sink and turned the tap. The cold water on his face was refreshing; it would grease the sleepy cracks in his face and wash his eyes clear.

He decided to drive the stolen Explorer to the village shopping center where he could get some coffee and a bite to eat. He hadn't eaten in almost 24 hours. He would try to call Harry as soon as the electricity came back on.

He stacked the written account of his story into a neat pile and stuffed the manuscript into an oversized envelope which he had addressed to Lorraine at her Treasury Department office in Washington DC. He felt safe for the moment.

Hugo and William most certainly had perished in the car accident last night. Dr. Trent would be short two trusted henchmen and unlikely to take any immediate action ... or she might even flee the country.

She was so confident that Dave's essence would be deleted. She had told him too much about her organization and that was a mistake that would have to be corrected. He would be in grave danger unless he could expose her to the authorities. He still had no evidence and no proof of anything that happened.

Perhaps he could inform Dr. Abramson of the experiments, but what could he do or say? He felt impotent ... every avenue of choice led to a dead end. He would think about it later after he'd had some coffee.

He drove to the main shopping area. The stores were still closed except for the coffee shop. He parked the Explorer. On the way to the coffee shop he spotted a mailbox outside the small post office. He made a mental note to come back after breakfast to buy postage and to mail the manuscript.

After two cups of coffee and a grilled breakfast ... thanks to a gas stove at the restaurant-coffee shop, he stood up to leave. There was a small waiting line; a couple of fisherman couldn't come up with the cash to pay for their breakfast. The credit card machines and computer registers were down. Cash was king in a world without electricity ... plastic would regain its throne when the lights came back on.

The waitress told the men to forget it for now and to come back later to pay the bill. It was a friendly place and most of the residents knew each other. Luckily, Dave had cash.. Suddenly the hum of power filled the room. Lights, music, refrigerators ... all came to life.

He headed for the phone outside the coffee shop, but three other people got there first. If only that cellular didn't have a lock code, he thought. It was 7:35 AM and the post office wouldn't be open until 8 AM. He decided to wait in the Explorer. He closed his eyes.

A sharp tapping sound on the driver's window startled Dave from a sound sleep. "You O.K. in there, Mister?" He rubbed his eyes to wipe away the fog. The bright sunlight made his eyes squint so he would be able to see the middle-aged man on the outside of the glass. Dave pressed the window switch and the glass sank into the door.

"You O.K., Mister?" the man said again.

"Yeah. I must have dozed off. Thanks for asking."

"Well, I'm sorry to wake you, but I wouldn't feel right not checking to see if you had a medical problem or something. Bye!" He turned and walked into the crowded shopping center.

Cars filled most of the parking spaces and the sidewalk was crowded with shoppers. Where did all the people come from so quickly. A few minutes ago the place was ... His eyes caught the time on the dash clock; it was 11:30 AM. Shit! I've been asleep for almost 4 hours. The post office; mail the manuscript, he thought. He started to open the door.

The pinhead-size red flashing red light caught his eye. The cellular phone was blinking; under the light was the word 'messages' and a button. He picked up the phone and pressed the button. "You have two messages." the monotone computer voice said. "Press 1 to play messages ... Press 2 to hold messages ..." He pressed 1.

"Hello, Dave! You know who this is ..." His legs stiffened, pressing into the floor board of the car, as he heard the sound of Dr. Trent's voice. "You were very lucky last night. The Highway Patrol contacted my office to break the news; the car Hugo and William were driving is registered to the Temple. They both died, of course

"I don't believe I can do anything for them, but how about you, Dave? Would you like a free ride into your second life when the time comes? Do you know what's better than life insurance, Dave? AfterLife insurance! ... Why don't we talk? Call me. The cell phone unlock code is 123; I have always had a bad memory for numbers ... call the word ETERNAL ... it's my direct personal number..." The line beeped, and then the computer voice spoke again.

"Saturday, 6:15 AM. Press 'messages' for your next message." He did.

Again the voice of Dr. Trent, saying "Dave, it's your doctor again. You haven't called. It's possible you've abandoned the car ... or you haven't noticed the message light. We have to talk. I can't allow you to jeopardize my organization's operations ... millions are at stake.

"By the way, I have canceled the order from the German Industrialist for the present ... We can't talk this out on the phone ... Come back to the 'Springs'. I had a surprise visitor this morning; Lorraine is here waiting for you." The line beeped.

"Press 1 to replay messages ... Press 2 to save messages ... Press 3 to erase messages ... Press 4 to record a new message ..." He hung up the phone as he spoke to himself out loud.

'Lorraine ... How the hell did she get Lorraine?' ... He turned the ignition key. The engine screamed and the tires screeched as he raced back to the 'Springs'.

He looked at Lorraine's body lying so still on the table ... or was it Lorraine?

CHAPTER 17

RETURN TO DANGER

"Harry, this is Dave!"

"Dave! Where the hell are you? I thought you might have been one of the men in that car accident last night. The police were still checking around the airport about you and thought there might be a connection to the men from the spa."

"Harry, I don't have time to explain. Just left Big Bear ... on my way back to the 'Springs'. Dr. Trent is Mr. Raven and they've got Lorraine! I'll explain everything later ... where are you?"

"I'm at my office. I called Lorraine yesterday as you asked. She flew into LA late last night because she was worried about you and then when we got that call from the Highway Patrol about 6 AM, she took a shuttle flight to the 'Springs' ... She went to the spa ... looking for you."

"Damn it!, Harry! She's in great danger. Dr. Trent is a killer!"

"I'll get on the phone and call the police!"

"No! That won't work. She won't kill her, she'll do worse ... but I don't think she will do anything until I get there. I'm sending you the whole story by FedX. I'll stop off and mail it to your club in LA ... Someone might try to intercept your office mail. It's a fantastic story! If anything happens to me or Lorraine, Print it!"

"Dave, I don't think this is a good idea ... let's try ..." Dave hung up on Harry and dialed 'ETERNAL'.

"Dave? Is it you?" spoke the voice of Dr. Trent.

"Yes! I'm on my way back. Put Lorraine on the phone." There was a short moment of silence as he waited to hear Lorraine's voice.

"Dave, it's me, Lorraine. Are you all right?"

"Yes, I'm fine."

"Dr. Trent said you'll be here in a couple of hours?"

"What are you doing there, Lorraine?"

"I thought something had happened to you. I had to come down to see for myself. ... The place is fabulous! And now that I know you're O.K., I'm going to enjoy it. Dr. Trent has offered to give me a free beauty treatment. I'm supposed to go in there now, they're waiting for me. I'll see you when you get here."

"Lorraine!! Wait! Don't ..."

Dr. Trent's voice came back on the line. "Hello, Dave. Don't worry. We'll take very good care of Lorraine; she has a beautiful body. I would kill to have her body." The phone went dead again. Dave raced toward the 'Springs', making a plan in his mind as he drove.

After he mailed the package to Harry, he drove to the spa ... parking in the rear. The storm had left traces of its ferocity from the night before. In the daylight he could see the palm tree that had been struck by lightning, Dr. Trent's private entrance, and the hillside he almost ran into. The lot was filled with mud and sagebrush.

He left the car and walked toward the door ... the sun was hot now ... directly overhead. He tried the door handle, but it was locked. He found the right key on Dr. Trent's keyring. He cautiously opened the door and walked into the small hallway and toward Dr. Trent's office.

He entered the room; it was empty. He bolted through the large door ... looking in both directions down the long hall. He ran toward the operating room. Fiona met him midway. "This way, Mr. Conway." she pointed to a narrow bronze doorway.

She pressed the access panel with the palm of her hand ... access by way of biometrics. The door slid open, revealing Lorraine lying on a recovery table bandaged in gauze wraps with tubes leading to her head. He ran toward her yelling, "What have you bastards done to her? Lorraine can you hear me? It's Dave!" She didn't move.

As he turned back to Fiona, she pressed her palm to the access panel ... the door slid shut, locking him in.

He charged at the closing door, "Fiona! ... Where is Dr. Trent? What have you done? " He beat on the bronze door with his fist. Then threw his shoulder up against the heavy door. He slid down to the floor in a sitting position; his back leaning into the door.

He looked at Lorraine lying so still on the table. ... or was it Lorraine? He screamed out, "No o o o o o o ......!!" Then he heard Dr. Trent's voice. Thank God!, he thought, and jumped to his feet. "Dr. Trent!" he yelled.

The TV screen mounted on the high corner wall revealed Dr. Trent's face. "Hello, David."

"What have you done to Lorraine? I'll kill you! ... I have written a full account of your horrible experiments. ... I ..." It took him a moment to realize that he wasn't seeing a live transmission. Dr. Trent was still talking over him. He could see the camera pulling back, showing a wide angle of the familiar operating room.

Lorraine was on the operating table. Her body was strapped down and the same head restraint they had attempted to use on him now held her head tightly in place.

He moved slowly toward the corner of the room, trying to get a closer and more detailed look at the screen. The electric probes were already sunk into her skull and brain. His pounding heart beat with rage as he continued to watch the horror of what he knew was to come.

Dr. Trent walked over to Lorraine, touching her as she spoke. "As you can see, David, the operation has begun. Fiona has been trained in the procedure and has done several successful transfers. You will note the other table that has already been prepared.

Lorraine's essence will be drained from her brain, and mine will be transferred to the computer and then directly into Lorraine's brain for chemical reconstitution of my essence."

No! You bitch! Stop! he screamed.

"Don't give up hope, Dave. You can still save her." He held his breath ... and waited. "Her essence will be stored; not deleted. When Lorraine awakes ... I mean when I awake from the transfer, you will do nothing. You will tell no one what you have seen or heard here.

"No doubt you have already told the entire story to your publisher, Harry Chrysler. He must not publish it. You will see that he does not ... or I will delete Lorraine's essence and you yourself will have killed her.

"I will leave the country and reorganize somewhere in Europe. You can't stop this, Dave. It's coming. Science will always continue to advance, making new discoveries. If I didn't discover the process, someone else would have. Don't try to moralize the right and wrong of it. You might even want to be a client some day.

"In three months it will be impossible to trace my whereabouts. If, in that time, you have withheld the story from the world, I will send Lorraine back to you ... whole and undamaged ... herself again. And now you are free to leave. Fiona will see you out. Good-bye, Dave." She went over to the table and laid down.

She lay on her back as Fiona made the preparations. She turned her head to the camera, holding a remote control in her hand. "You have to trust me, Dave. You have no choice." She pointed the remote at the screen and it went blank.

She had won! What could he do? He would have to trust her ... to wait ... If she didn't keep her word, he would spend the rest of his life hunting her down. He would find her and expose her to the world ... or kill her. His thoughts were interrupted by the sound of moans coming from Lorraine's body.

He turned from the TV monitor and walked toward her stirring body. He wanted to hold her. No ... strangle her! His racing mind was confused. He was frustrated with both grief and anger at the same time.

He couldn't help himself; he embraced the body that was Lorraine, and held her tightly, rocking to and fro, repeating her name over and over again. Lorraine! ... Lorraine! I love you! Her eyelids began to flutter and then open as she spoke, "Dave ... Dave"

"Shut up, you bitch! Don't talk!" he yelled. He took her by the shoulders as she started to sit up. "Shut up! Shut up! You fucking bitch!"

"Dave, Dave. What happened? Where am I?"

"You know damn well where you are. I could strangle you for what you've done to my Lorraine." He grabbed her by the throat.

"Dave, Honey! Cut that out! Stop, I said." She grabbed his hands. His mouth opened to speak as she yelled out, "Now hush up and tell me what's happened? What the hell is going on? What did Dr. Trent do to me; I've got the mother of all hangovers ..." She grabbed her head, feeling around the gauze bandages. She let out a howling yell!

The TV monitor came back to life showing Fiona in the operating room with Dr. Trent's unconscious body lying on the table. Lorraine's body was no where in sight. Fiona spoke to the camera. "I did not make the transfer. I withdrew Dr. Trent's essence into the computer and erased it. She is just an empty shell. You will want to know why I have done this. I have lived in fear that she would some day kill me after I had served her purpose. I was in her power. The yearly medications I had to take to stay alive, made me her slave. I couldn't run away.

"Now, today, she gave me the opportunity to free myself … to escape her cruelty. I knew I might never have another chance to save myself. I'm leaving the temple. I know the medications I need to stay alive. I have saved your Lorraine, now you must not come after me. I have set the lock timer on the door for 15 minutes. It will unlock automatically. You should take Lorraine to a medical facility as soon as possible. Her brain is undamaged but she must be observed for 72 hours."

The bronze door slid open. He looked at Lorraine and knew he would have a lot of explaining to do.

Now that I have written the ending to this story, I can concentrate on Lorraine whom I thought I had lost forever. And now that I have her back I'll never take a chance on losing her again.

The hospitals in Palm Springs are among the best in the world. If you're going to have a heart attack or stroke, this is probably one of the safest towns in America to have it. The wealthy require the best medical facilities and the top talents of heart specialists and neurosurgeons. So Lorraine had the best.

After three days she was given her release, and an expensive clean bill of health. The surgical evidence of her operation was quite difficult to explain to the doctors. I left that up to Dr. Abramson, who will be working with us on publishing the story. Harry was delighted with the arrangement.

Outside, packing the luggage into a cab in the hospital parking lot, and in the midday heat, I said to Lorraine. "I'm moving back East until you can get transferred back to California."

"That's wonderful, Honey! This way you can work at home and watch the kids while I'm at the office." We kissed and hugged.

"Wait a minute, Lorraine!" I said as I took her by the shoulders and looked deeply into those beautiful eyes.. "I'm pretty sure that's you in there, but I need to know for sure."

"O.K., Dave, but this is a 'helavuh time to find out."

"How much did we pay for that couch we both love so much, that you now keep in your living room? She stood silent ... puzzled? Not able to answer, I thought. My heart skipped a beat.

"Well, for heaven's sake. What a question! We bought it at an auction. It belonged to a famous Washington senator."

"Thanks, Baby! I needed that!" We hugged and kissed again.

She looked into my eyes as she spoke in a more sober tone. "Dave, I've been thinking ... about Dr. Trent. Do you suppose she might be right about a lot of those things you told me? ... the future of medical transplants? ... and rebirths?"

"Lorraine, I read the answer to that question at the end of the diary, 'Our business is our time; the future will have to take care of itself.'"

I heard myself say the words, but I couldn't help feel that Dr. Trent and Dr. Abramson were right about the secrets of life being out there like buried treasure waiting to be discovered by saints or medical pirates.

The urge to live is the strongest of our human instincts, yet men and women have given their lives to save others. They have made the ultimate sacrifice ... without hesitation or regret. It is an unnatural contradiction that makes our race totally unpredictable and that is mankind's best defense against moral greed and corruption.

"Nobly to live or
Else nobly to die
Befits proud birth."

Sophocles   495-405 B

Coming Soon;
  another page-turning **novel** by
  Raymond Thor.

Murder is Inconsiderate©

mystery, suspense, adventure, ...

A 100-year-old jewel theft threads its curse down through the years via royalty and Al Capone to a murder in present day NY city. A burnt-out homicide detective, who's walking the fence between good cop or rich cop, forms an alliance with the prime suspect, a beautiful insurance investigator, who is every bit his 'bitch for bastard' match.

The victim was transporting the jewels, which are missing and somehow connected to the nuclear defense of the Mediterranean.

Clues lead them on a course of harrowing escapes, erotica, and mystery as they run afoul of thieves, mercenaries and CIA.

Everyone is suspect as they meet in a final collective conflict of pursuit, murder, and plot twist: 'Who did it?', and 'Who is going to do it to whom?'

Copyright: WGAw

MAIL ORDER TO:

email: **www.dangerpub.com**

DANGER PUBLISHING
1014 S. Westlake Blvd • Suite 14-155
Westlake Village CA 91361

Please fill in all information

name _____

address _____

city, state, zip _____

phone _____

FOR A GIFT TO SOMEONE SPECIAL, REQUEST AN AUTOGRAPHED COPY DIRECT FROM THE PUBLISHER.

Hardcover (ISBN 0-9658727-7-7) $23.95

Softcover (ISBN 0-9658727-6-9) $14.95

CA resident add 7.25% sales tax   **Number of copies** ____

Raymond Thor, Author

All his life a great storyteller, Ray has always come up with tales and adventures which he then turns into a form of reality for all his five children. He resides in Southern CA and writes both novels and screenplays.

His next mystery novel, MURDER IS INCONSIDERATE, is due in 1998.

http://www. dangerpub.com

Copyright © 1997
First Printing 1997 USA

ISBN 0-9658727-7-7
LCCN 97-68244

PUBLISHED BY: First Edition
DANGER PUBLISHING

1014 S. Westlake Blvd • Suite 14-155
Westlake Village   CA   91361 USA

Reg. WGAw